Hooky's
Big Egg!

Quillquest Books

USA

Quillquest Books

A division of the Quillquest Publishing Co., USA
Quillquest Books, Quillquest Junior Books,
Quillquest Classic Books, and the sailing quill are the exclusive
trademarks of the Quillquest Publishing Co, USA.
For information or comments about this book contact
Quillquestbooks@msn.com

ISBN-10: 0-940075-26-1
ISBN-13: 978-0-940075-26-9
Copyright © 2018 by Frank Mosco
Cover Copyright © 2018 by Quillquest Books

Visit the author's web site at: www.frankmosco.com

For

My good friend Jimmy Carter

A Note from the Author

Believe it or not I actually have some friends. Not lots and lots of friends such as, say, authors Clive Cussler or Stephen King. Stephen King loves to write about strange things and strange people (from the dark side) and somehow still manages to accumulate lots of friends. You would think that someone who is way out there like Stephen King would chase off potential friends, but no, he just keeps raking them in like he does money. Just the same, I do have some friends and I value the friends I do have. And that's why I'm posting this particular note as a warning to my friends. It's not that I don't care about the readers I don't know, but I just happen to care more about the ones I do know, most of whom know me well enough to know not to read my books while in church on Sunday… or in church on any other day. The warning is this:

* CAUTION *

THIS BOOK HAS SOME NASTY WORDS. THESE WORDS ARE ALSO KNOWN AS CURSE WORDS. THEY ARE THE WORDS THAT WOULD CAUSE YOUR MOTHER TO WASH YOUR MOUTH OUT WITH SOAP OR SLAP YOUR ASS SIX WAYS TO SUNDAY. SO HEED THIS WARNING; **IF YOU ARE A PRUDE, A PRIEST, OR SOMEWHAT QUEASY ABOUT *NASTY WORDS* THEN BE PREPARED TO SEE SOME OF THESE *NASTY WORDS* WHEN YOU READ THIS BOOK, AND UNDERSTAND THAT IT'S ALL IN GOOD FUN. I MEAN, AFTER ALL, DAMN, WHO REALLY GIVES A SHIT, RIGHT?**

And there it is, you have been warned so please don't send me any letters or e-mails to tell me you didn't like the "nasty words" (or sexual references) and that you are praying for my soul and forgiveness, or that you hope I burn in hell for being so profane and despicable while being so funny. You wouldn't do that to Stephen King would you? Of course not.

Oh yeah, and thanks to everyone who helped but won't admit they had anything to do with the publishing of this novel, especially those proofers who think I got my grammatical education in a tree - you are much appreciated… damn it.

Hooky's
Big Egg!

By

Frank Mosco

Prologue

1958
The Big Round French Thing

Hooky Chua Lotta stood buck ass naked and totally amazed as he watched the giant white round thing being lowered by the huge red crane into the big hole. To Hooky it looked like a giant egg, and to Hooky the egg was an amazing sight to see with blinking lights and probes and wires extending out in all directions. So many in fact, that it reminded him of his third wife's hair. Hooky never really liked his third wife's hair and in fact didn't even want to marry his third wife in the first place, but her father wanted to get rid of her so badly that he gave Hooky two pigs as part of the deal. Hooky thought two wives was already a pain in the ass, but what the hell; pigs were hard to come by that year and were in high demand. Later, however, Hooky decided he had gotten a good bargain, not because he received two pigs but because his third wife turned out to be pretty damn good in the sack and when you toss in his other two wives it was that much better. Also she really knew how to whip up a damn good pig roast.

Just why all those Frenchmen thought that big round thing Hooky now referred to as the *big egg* was so important was beyond him, and why these white guys were using a crane to place it in the big hole on his beautiful tropical island out in the middle of the Pacific Ocean was beyond his reasoning. After all, Hooky was not an unintelligent man and had no problem realizing that a few good men with little effort could just as easily roll that big ass egg right into that big ass hole. After all, thought Hooky, most all things round will roll. It was simple island physics; if it looks like a coconut and is round like a coconut, then the damn thing should roll like a coconut. A lesson Hooky learned as a child playing on the beach with his friends - and coconuts.

Hooky didn't know much about all these white guys puttering around and treating this big egg like it was some kind of religious experience, but he did know they had a lot of fascinating technology and he was taking it all in like some little kid on his first visit to the circus. All he knew was this big ass egg was important enough or secret enough for all these white guys to make all of his people leave the island and start living on some other island that was so far away he couldn't even paddle there in his dugout canoe.

Hooky had never seen large ships and equipment like this before except for that time in a canoe when a Japanese destroyer tried to run him over. That was back in 1942. And those rude Japanese were laughing at him the entire time. Hooky remembered it well because it takes a long time to make a dugout canoe and the one he was in belonged to his grandfather and his grandfather was a total dick. If the Japs had run him down it would mean Hooky's grandfather would have blamed him and he would have had to build his grandfather a new dugout canoe. Not a very appealing thought for Hooky because basically Hooky was too damn lazy to even think about building a canoe or anything else. That's why he was using his grandfather's canoe in the first place. Hooky was what you might call an Island Renaissance Man, a thoughtful kind of guy. He realized that if smashing his grandfather's canoe happened now it wouldn't be a problem because now he has three wives and four kids who could chop on that sucker for days, knocking out a new canoe in no time and still manage to come up with dinner. Hell, he thought, they could even chop down the tree they would need to make it in the first place. Not that any of that mattered anyhow because his grandfather died two years ago.

Hooky originally thought since he, along with a few other native men, were chosen to remain on the island that it was an honor that demonstrated his obvious exceptional intelligence, but eventually that theory, the fun and games, and his curiosity about the French began to wear thin. It turned out that he and his island brothers were there just to cater to the needs of all these strange white guys who ate weird food and drank a lot of wine.

Hooky didn't think their behavior was such a big deal at first, after all he wasn't one to criticize anyone's preferred diet, but on the other hand he certainly wasn't going to accept their personal hygiene… or lack of.

It seems all those white guys had a peculiar scent about them that just curdled in Hooky's nose and he sure as hell didn't like being chosen to empty their shit pots and wash their clothes no matter what kind of goodies they bribed him with. And why would anyone want to wear clothes in the first place? Hell, thought Hooky, this is women's work, not something for a well mannered lazy Island Renaissance Man like himself. He quickly realized that whatever that stuff was they were consuming smelled ten times worse on the way out as it did on the way in and that was saying a lot because what they ate was just plain gross before they even ate it. Why the hell can't they just shit in the surf like everybody else thought Hooky and his island brothers? And to think that Hooky and the islanders gave themselves a special tattoo in the form of a feathered egg just for the sake of honoring this important occasion and their association with these strange white French guys.

So now there he was, one of the few original residents of his island who was still *on* his island, observing with amazement a group of white foreigners playing with a giant egg while they drank stuff that tasted like rotten coconut milk and pig piss, ate smelly shit that turned into even worse smelling shit, and spoke like drunken sea gulls in a language Hooky hadn't heard since he was a boy. It was back when a couple of nuns showed up on their island, moved in, and tried to teach him and all his island relatives how to dress, speak, and pray; something in which none of his people had any interest mainly because all the people on Hooky's island were perfectly comfortable going naked, speaking their own language, and sure as hell didn't want to talk to some almighty mystery dude up in space who they couldn't see and never talked back or answered any of their questions. The ordeal with the nuns was eventually remedied when the older men of the island won them over and converted them to group sex. Soon after, the nuns returned to France to convert others into their newly discovered group sex religious sect and the last anyone heard the nuns' newly formed holy sect was growing with leaps and bounds, especially after they opened a branch in a place called San Francisco on a big island called America.

The only other time Hooky was exposed to any foreign languages was in 1943 during WWII when a Japanese freighter full of international prisoners ran aground in a storm. The assortment of nearly two hundred prisoners and three Japanese soldiers were a mix of nearly every existing nationality and this offered up a smorgasbord of confusing dialects. Many of the survivors were frail and sickly and died soon after their arrival. Those twenty plus who survived were taken in and fed and nursed back to health by Hooky's native tribesmen. After which the survivors, now being strong and healthy and having no love for their Japanese captors, wasted no time killing all three soldiers. Many of those survivors even seemed to enjoy the Polynesian style luau at which the natives of the island celebrated and danced naked. And the Japanese were served up as the main course along with assorted fish, pig, fruit, and coconut jam. They were particularly pleased when they got a taste of the island special sauce called *funglu*.

Funglu is a mysterious combination of indigenous island herbs mixed with the blood of a rare yellow fish, the crushed eyes of a local lizard for good luck, and a very special blossom of a wild flower that grows on the mountain, all in a bowl of sweet coconut milk and a certain human body fluid known only to the chosen few who are authorized to produce it. It is a mixture that also acts as a very potent fast and lasting natural aphrodisiac and it's that special sauce that accounts for the islanders' culture which values and prizes group sex. Exposed to all this, the survivors forgot about eventually being rescued and returning to their various homelands of origin and eventually assimilated into Hooky's island tribe, thoroughly enjoying lots of funglu and group sex, all the while influencing the island language that evolved into a vernacular as difficult to decipher and understand as that of the Rosetta Stone, the US Tax Code, or the Obamacare website.

Hooky remembered those times well, especially that tasty funglu Japanese sushi which soon after was outlawed do to the scruples and influence of some of their more religious new residents, some of which even reminded Hooky of the nuns. But through the years as a few of those folks began to give in to the funglu and others passed away, the island people who had been using the funglu for generations came together and declared it a legal substance once again. The vote was unanimous.

One day while Hooky was collecting the French shit pots left from the night before, he noticed that some of the shit pots were empty and none of the white French guys were around and that even all the special weird Frenchmen who always seemed to be pouring over large sheets of paper on their big flat tables had disappeared. Concerned he was about to miss something important, Hooky quickly neglected the shit pots and ran to the site of the big egg. When he arrived he was surprised to discover all the Frenchmen standing around the big hole in the ground where sat the big egg. They all seemed very sad and perplexed and for the most part just stood and stared into the big hole. Occasionally one or two would speak softly to the one standing next to him and the one next to him would nod his head in agreement and throw his hand up in the air as if to say he had no idea what the other guy was talking about. At least that's how it appeared to Hooky. In truth the French technicians were debating and then voting on the future of the big egg.

Hooky slowly made his way to the edge of the big hole and looked down. There it lay with all its blinking lights and wires and probes and gizmos. All protruding and looking like his third wife's hair. And around it were all the Frenchmen standing, looking down on the big egg as though they were at a funeral. Finally the boss Frenchman, after somehow summing up the general consensus of the others, (and Hooky knew he was the boss because he never did any work and had the worse smelling shit pot of them all) raised his hand and yelled, *Nous sommes décidés. La bombe sera laissée derrière. Burry ça,* meaning, *We are decided. The bomb will be left behind. Burry that sucker.* Words Hooky did not understand. Suddenly the blinking lights on the big egg stopped blinking and the cable from the huge crane disconnected and easily came free of the big egg at the bottom of the big hole. Immediately the sound of a powerful grumbling machine approached and began pushing dirt into the hole and it continued until the giant egg was completely covered. Hooky watched as all the distressed Frenchmen slowly turned and walked away, grieving the end and loss of their six months of hard work.

"What is happening?" asked Hooky. But he was completely ignored.

The Frenchmen continued to dribble away so Hooky approached one of the last men leaving, tapped his shoulder and asked again, "What is happening. Where is everybody going?"

The French technician didn't understand a word Hooky said but could see by his concerned expression that he was in need of an answer. "Annulé. Le test a été annulé. Annulé. Le test a été annulé...

"I don't understand. What are you saying?" interrupted Hooky. But in a like manner the Frenchman didn't understand Hooky.

He began to repeat his answer to Hooky when he was suddenly interrupted and assisted by another technician. "Annulé. Le test a été…

"Cancelled," said the man in a chopped version of Hooky's language. "What he said to you was the test has been cancelled."

"Test?" asked Hooky. "What is a test?"

"Yes, the test. Of the bomb, the big bomb. It has been cancelled and we are leaving."

"What is a bomb and why did you burry it?" inquired Hooky.

"Because we don't know what to do with it," answered the French technician. "And we don't want to carry it around because it is very dangerous."

"You mean like a shit pot?"

"Um, yes something like that."

"You are leaving my island?"

"Yes, we are leaving the island. But we will likely return to complete our big bomb test um… or something… someday… maybe."

"My people can return?"

"I don't know. I only deal with the bomb. I don't know about your people. But…"

"But what…?" asked an anxious Hooky.

"If you ever return here remember…" said the Frenchman, "you must never ever dig that thing up and you should never ever touch it. Do you understand? *Never, never ever.*"

Hooky nodded his head letting the French technician know he understood even though he didn't understand at all. The deep sound of a ship's horn drifted through the palms sounding the order to board.

"Don't worry. We will take you to your people. Now we must hurry," said the Frenchman.

"To my wives? You will take me to my three wives and children?"

"Of course... Oh wait. You say you have three wives?"

"Yes, unfortunately I only have three," answered Hooky. "I have a small shelter and must also make room for my children and our pigs and birds. You know, for when the rains come."

"What do you do when the rains don't come?" inquired the Frenchman.

"Nothing. Why should I do anything? They are always well off and they come home when they are hungry and when it's time to feed the pigs."

"Hmm... I'm not sure if that's good or bad. Just the same we must now hurry and board the ship."

"I will hurry," replied Hooky and he ran off to gather his few belongings and inform his brother natives who were washing clothes and collecting shit pots to tell them that it was time for them to stop collecting shit pots and depart the island.

By the end of the day the French equipment and everyone on the island had been loaded aboard the ship moored just off shore. As it sailed away, Hooky and his island brothers stood on the deck and watched their island shrink away into the distance.

"We will come back," said Hooky to his fellow tribesmen. "The white French guys are going to take us to our families and then take us all back home."

What Hooky didn't know was in a time of national turmoil France was having a problem losing a war somewhere in Africa or Asia or both and General Charles André Joseph Marie de Gaulle, a French WWII hero who did nothing in WWII except give France to the Germans, came out of retirement to fix everything... or so he said. And to fix everything he founded the Fifth Republic with a strong presidency in the form of himself, and he did it so well that he was soon elected to continue in that role in perpetuity kind of like Napoleon Bonaparte except without killing a million French soldiers. The French people didn't really give a damn because the French, who never really give a damn about anything anyway and are as willing to celebrate as they are to lose wars, decided this establishment of a Fifth Republic was a good reason and a good time to celebrate and revel for a long time, maybe weeks, maybe months. Also because as long as they were celebrating, French law declared they were excused from work with pay. And so the big egg test technicians who got paid better than your average French croissant baker and pretty much everyone else in France, hurried home to do just that, revel with pay for an extended period of time.

Soon after, de Gaulle's new government defunded the big egg experiment in order to fund the new national party's party and cut pay checks for an entire nation of non-workers. As a result the big egg and the beautiful tropical island it was buried on were long forgotten. In fact, the French technicians who dearly missed their daily dose of frog legs, escargot, skinny bread, wine, and pastries were in such a big hurry to rush home and revel that they dropped Hooky and his tribal brothers off on the wrong island. Hooky was dismayed to discover this after the French ship departed and he soon became determined to find his family and take them home which is exactly what he did. The intrepid Hooky Chua Latta, like some Polynesian Moses, searched out the lost islanders after three long months and led them all back to their homes and their precious funglu.

Of course Hooky's quest wasn't a stroll in the park. The most difficult part of his ordeal was, once finding his people; he had to find a way to pay their passage to get them home. The solution came with a tramp steamer and the price came dear, but in his eyes it was well worth giving up his third wife as payment. She was led to believe she would soon be sent home after the debt was settled but the deal he made was with a dubious Greek Captain who was also a smuggler of war surplus weapons, women into slavery, and most anything else that would turn a dollar. Hooky resolved to accept this trade by seeing it simply as the loss of his two pig wife and an occasional good lay, something he could always replace.

Having his islanders settled on the tramp steamer for their journey home, Hooky decided to relieve their anxiety by relaying the fascinating story of all those odd Frenchmen, their strange food and drink habits, and of course their very stinky shit pots. He also relayed the story of the big egg. For experiencing all this and rescuing and taking his people home, just like General Charles André Joseph Marie de Gaulle, Hooky Chua Latta was awarded a custom made canoe and declared the Chief and Top Coconut Jam, Bread Fruit, and Funglu Distributor for life which gave him a great deal of power over the entire island. This was a fortunate act indeed because Hooky knew if he told all the residents of the island to stay away from the big egg as he was instructed by the departing Frenchman, undoubtedly they would all become curious as hell and dig the damn thing up, if for no other reason than to see if it actually did look like Hooky's third wife's hair. Therefore Hooky declared the big egg that was hidden deep in the big hole to be a sacred place. He declared it should be revered and feared and all the people were told to steer clear for fear of suffering a vengeance and incredibly vicious curse set on them from… the *Sacred Big Egg*.

And so it came to pass, on their beautiful tropical island somewhere out in the middle of the Pacific Ocean, Hooky Chua Latta, the Chief and Top Coconut Jam,

Bread Fruit, and Funglu Distributor in Perpetuity, (which also afforded him a small piece of the action), and his small tribe of island natives lived undisturbed and happy, all the while learning and speaking some of the language of the survivors of the WWII Jap cargo ship; a very strange mixed vocabulary that sounded like no other on the planet. For them there was no greater existence on earth. Here they could run around buck ass naked, consume large quantities of funglu, and have group sex on a regular basis without criticism. And even on rare occasions they would treat themselves to a luau featuring sushi made of deceased loved ones laced with funglu.

This was Hooky's plan... which of course did not include shit pots.

Chapter 1

60 Years Later
Popo YoYo

It was just another quiet tropical night on the island. The palm trees swayed with a warm lazy ocean breeze that rolled in above an easy constant surf. The few exotic birds that were yet to settle for the night were calling out to the full moon but somehow seemed to join in with the soft eloquent sound of melodic voices in song drifting across the island paradise. The islanders were gathered around a fire and singing, partly in celebration and partly in bereavement, because the old man had died. After many years of administering love and wisdom (and coconut jam, bread fruit, and funglu) to his people, Hooky Chua Latta had finally passed away while having group sex with his five wives.

"Where you will go, we do not know. Above the sea among the stars," were the words of the melodic song sung by the islanders. *"But we will be with you for all time and will someday share your journey. We will see*

you again on that magic island far away. May your journey there be one of joy and wonder."

That was the celebration part of the ceremony. The sorrow part of the ceremony was they had all agreed not to have the traditional luau with lots of Hooky sushi and funglu. It was a difficult decision to make because having such a tradition was their way of honoring their lost relatives that they actually liked and loved. All others, the dicks and disagreeable ones like Hooky's grandfather, were usually just tossed to the sharks off the big cliff above the south shore. The islanders firmly believed in the philosophy of, *"you are what you eat."* But on this occasion they had all decided their love and affection for Hooky was stronger, something altogether different, and that Hooky was so special in life that he deserved something very special in death and they wanted him to stay with them in body as well as spirit. For this they agreed that Hooky should be placed in permanent memorial atop his famous big egg to hopefully gain favor with the sacred thing and, of course, hoping to avoid getting cursed or messed up during the process of placing him there. They felt that in some way Hooky would protect them.

And so they did exactly that; choosing to secure their future safety from Hooky's dangerous Amazing Big Egg by feeding it Hooky and erecting on the same spot a big twelve foot tall Kahuna memorial in his liking (although it actually looked more like a totem pole with the face of a demon from Hell). Rather than having the traditional luau with Hooky sushi and funglu they instead draped his memorial with flowers and gifts and island leis. Having survived that process without being cursed or screwed up they now sat facing the communal fire and sang with both joy and sorrow, all the while wishing they had some sushi and funglu. Suddenly when they ceased singing the full moon crawled behind a cloud and all became quiet and dark over the entire island. The fire spit large quantities of sparks into the sky and the islanders looked about into the darkness, up into the trees and at each other, shaking their heads and wondering what was happening. Then suddenly all the birds of the island awakened and began squawking and screaming. When the moon came from behind the clouds the birds took to the sky in wild desperate flight. The islanders watched and wondered if this was a good or a bad omen and most importantly… had they angered Hooky's Amazing Big Egg to the point it was now about to destroy them and their homes. Indeed, to possibly swallow them into the dark depths where resides Hooky's mysterious egg!

Everyone turned to Popo YoYo who was the next in line to rule the island because he was the grandson of Hooky and Hooky's two pig third wife with the crazy hair. Also because he was the most informed in regards to the big egg which made him seem to be a very wise man. Popo YoYo was fully informed because Hooky told him the true story of the big egg each and every night of his life, (except on funglu nights when he or they were involved in traditional group sex). Hooky did this for two reasons; first of all Popo YoYo was very good at keeping secrets and second because Hooky always felt guilty about giving away Popo YoYo's two pig grandmother. And so now all the islanders looked to Popo YoYo for an answer to belay their new found anxiety regarding the strange events taking place around them.

Popo YoYo looked about prudently as though he was completely in charge of events, of which of course he wasn't, a trait he also learned from Hooky; how to be in charge when you actually weren't. He then turned and quickly sprinted into the darkness in the direction of the big kahuna Hooky memorial above the site of the buried big egg. The earth beneath his feet began to shake as he ran along causing him to fall. He quickly rose and wrapped himself around a coconut tree in panic as the earth's shaking and trembling grew more intense. *"What's happening?"* thought Popo YoYo. *"Could it be true? Have we angered Hooky's Amazing Big Egg? Is it going to destroys us?"*

Back at the campfire the islanders began to panic, children screamed and old people moaned. Their new leader had run off and left them and now the island was going to swallow them up because they had angered the big egg… or so they thought.

Meanwhile, Popo YoYo screwed up his courage and decided to continue to his grandfather's memorial to challenge the big egg or to at least take the opportunity to call his grandfather a big fat liar. All around him the earth rumbled, huge boulders rolled down hills from the nearby mountain, plowing over and through trees to nearly miss squashing Popo YoYo. Once again he fell to the ground only to look up just in time to move out of the way of a falling bolder. He jumped up and desperately continued making his way to Hooky's big kahuna memorial when suddenly the earth shook and rose under him with a tremendous deep rumble. The boulders and fallen trees were lifted off the ground and the waterfall that ran so prominently from the top of the mountain stopped altogether then began falling from the top of the mountain from another place. Popo YoYo watched all this in amazement as he continued.

Finally Popo YoYo arrived at the high mound of ground that was the burial site of his grandfather and the big egg. He paused and stared, not sure what to expect, then began to slowly approach as he yelled, "Oh Amazing Big Egg here me now. I am Popo YoYo, grandson of Hooky Chua Lotta and Two Pig third wife. I come to beg your forgiveness for what we have done and ask what we must do to make all things right again, to appease you and quell your anger?"

Popo YoYo watched and waited while the island rumbled and shook all around him. The wind blew and the birds screamed and the ground rose and fell and formed large crevasses. Then suddenly the earth shook even more violently beneath him and he fell to his knees in fear, all the while watching his grandfather's big kahuna memorial and the shaking large mound on which it stood. Now sure he was going to die Popo YoYo yelled, "Grandfather Hooky Chua Latta! Grandfather Hooky hear me now as I say to you… I say… you are full of shit and I will never forgive you for selling two pig grandmother to that lying Greek. And not only that, I'm going to tell all the islanders that you emptied more French shit pots than any other brother."

Just then the ground rolled and the mound covering the big egg began to swell and expand and in the center at the top the earth opened up and out popped the dead Hooky Chua Latta all wrapped and dressed and looking nicer than he had in his last twenty years. Up he came and oddly enough his body stood and leaned against the big kahuna pole as though it was standing on its own. This time however he looked much different than when they had put him in the ground. This time Hooky Chua Latta seemed to… glow in the dark.

"Oh wow!" said Popo YoYo. "I must have really, really pissed him off. Oops."

Then just as suddenly, the shaking earth ceased and all became calm once again. The wild winds stopped and the birds returned to their nesting places except for one, an old toucan, the one that used to sit atop Hooky's grass hut, now sat perched atop the big kahuna memorial. Popo YoYo rose and faced Hooky Chua Latta's glowing remains and could find no words to express his feelings. When he finally turned he discovered that behind him all the islanders had also come to beg forgiveness from the big egg and they had witnessed Popo YoYo's brave challenge and the rise and shine of their beloved Hooky.

Among them was a young girl by the name of Bertha Moo Mojo. Bertha had an Anglo first name because she was the descendent of an American sailor who was among the prisoners from the wrecked Japanese ship in 1944. The now deceased sailor's name was George and he was exceptionally fond of funglu which resulted in a long line of Berthas, in fact he was heavy into the funglu up until the day he died at age 83. George always insisted on naming his offspring with Anglo names and demanding they all learn his language. George's problem however was that due to so much group sex the islanders were never really sure whose offspring was whose offspring, but then they didn't really care one way or the other because they all took care of each other from birth. And so on occasion George would just pick one if it had any amount of resemblance to his blonde self and if it were a girl name her Bertha after his mother back in the Bronx of New York. Nobody actually cared because it was part of their culture to let the children choose their own names whenever they felt like it. So it was fine with everyone that George did his own thing except for the fact that George's language was somewhat colorful and resulted in a line of children who cursed like sailors which of course eventually worked its way into the island daily vernacular… but then nobody really noticed.

"Holy shit!" exclaimed Bertha. "Did you guys see that? That old fucker just shot up outta the dirt and lit up like a bunch of tiki torches. God damn, that's more incredible than a Saigon whore on opium," she said in her odd mix of island and Anglo sailor lingo.

"What does that mean?" asked an islander.

"It means our new fuckin' king has got his shit together is what it means," answered Bertha.

"No. I mean what is opium?"

"Shit if I know," replied Bertha. "I just know our new king kicks ass better than an unhappy mule."

"What's that mean?"

"What's what mean?" asked Bertha.

"A mule. What's a mule."

"Hell if I know," replied Bertha.

"Yes," said another. "He has challenged Hooky's Big Egg and became victorious and saved our lives and our island. Hurrah for Popo YoYo! Hurrah for our new king! All honor Popo YoYo, Chief and Top Coconut Jam, Bread Fruit, and Funglu Distributor in Perpetuity!"

And they all went to their knees and bowed their heads to Popo YoYo who gave a cursory nod in return then

33

turned back to the glowing mummy leaning against the big kahuna monument who was his grandfather and said with great authority the essence of, "Let's get the hell out of here before we all start glowing in the dark."

"But why would we glow in the dark?" asked an islander.

"Oh you know… just in case, I mean," answered a hesitant Popo YoYo.

"But what about that old fart?" asked Bertha.

"He's not going anywhere," replied Popo YoYo.

"Oh, okay," said Bertha. "Um, what was that you were saying about shit pots?"

Chapter 2

Tex the Big Bopper

In the center of a large luxurious conference room stood a fifteen foot long oval hand crafted imported rosewood table inlaid with gold and pearl emblems depicting the corporate logo and the various holdings of the Texas Yellow Rose Corporation. The logo consisted of the face of a mean looking longhorn steer with a big yellow rose on its forehead. The table was lined with small gold plated lamps with Tiffany shades. Above the table hung two very large chandeliers made of elk antlers with gold light fixtures hung from each point of each antler. On the table at each of the high back soft kangaroo leather chairs sat a leather notebook containing the night's meeting agenda as well as other pertinent information and a small menu to be filled in case the meeting ran long and dinner was to be served. The contents of each folder were written in the language necessary to cater to the individual to be seated at that particular chair. There also sat a small pad of blank paper and a gold pen along with a crystal glass and pitcher filled with imported glacier water. A few of the settings included containers of individually preferred liquors as requested by the attendee. Next to each glass sat a small dish containing lime slices, mints, and a silk napkin. The contents at each seat signified that on this day the table was prepped for a very important meeting involving some very important people who had traveled from all around the world for this particular occasion.

At present the room was empty except for one occupant who stood near a large window across the room, a tall lanky man with a grey goatee wearing a custom western style suit with fringes, rattlesnake boots, and a custom broad brimmed Stetson cowboy hat that he never removed except when he was taking a dump in his executive restroom or when he was having sex. He is Tommy "Tex" Drake, known more widely around the world and in the oil business as "Tex the Big Bopper." The Big Bopper handle came years ago when Tex came face to face with a Bengal tiger on a hunting trip in India. His Indian guide had handed him an unloaded rifle when he was ready to shoot the critter and by the time the guide corrected his mistake and started to hand Tex the loaded weapon the tiger decided to attack. In true Texas form the long tall Tommy "Tex" Drake threw a serious Duke Wayne cross hook and bopped the ferocious animal dead cold, then shot him. The Indians turned him into a legend saying he *bopped* the tiger dead. It was then that Tex gained his nickname Big Bopper, but also lost two fingers on the Tigers sharp choppers.

Tex the Big Bopper was standing and staring out of the large window of his natural oak wood paneled conference room on the top floor of his ten stories corporate headquarters in the primo business district of Dallas. He looked below and observed impatiently as the various limousines arrived delivering the board member/investors of his massive financial enterprise. He had called this meeting because he had some bad news and some very important good news, and regardless of what the board members had to say, Tex the Big Bopper was about to let them know they were going to branch into an entirely new business.

When each board member was escorted into the room and seated at the immaculate table, Tex the Big Bopper reviewed in his mind his assessment of each of their profiles. First to arrive was Congresswoman Mary Pintada of California. Mary Pintada had been a member of the US House of Representatives for many years and likewise a board member of Tex's company for quite a few years as well. To Tex, Mary was way short on brains but long on influence. She had also married big money decades ago which Tex had milked for investment into his business, and as long as he continued to pay good dividends stupid Mary was always along for the ride. In addition she was attractive and had a nice ass of which he often took for a ride as well, and which she used in a true Democratic way in the swamp of Washington to persuade our legislators to vote her way, a way that most often was Tex's way. Tex once thought of running her for President but unfortunately she couldn't carry on a press conference without appearing as though she was high on oxycodone or a steady diet of Persian poppies.

Next to enter the room was the filthy rich Bubba Jon Jones who gained all his wealth prospecting in Oklahoma. While chipping away at some rocks on the side of a cliff in the Wichita Mountains, Bubba Jon slipped and fell thirty-seven feet and landed safely in a pool of crude oil. Since Bubba Jon always had the habit of filing a claim on the land he was about to prospect he discovered that his claim also included all minerals and forms of petroleum. The state of Oklahoma quickly realized their mistake and the fact that due to Bubba's claim they had lost billions of dollars in oil revenue so they changed the rule that allowed anyone to file claims on unproven ground and required they state specifically what the claim was for. They also made it illegal to file prior claims anywhere where they couldn't get their hands on it first which was just about everywhere. As if that weren't enough, the marvelous minds of State Government fired Stella Rodriguez Fosgate, the poor girl who wrote, accepted, and filed the claim on behalf of Bubba Jon Jones who couldn't read and also because at the state's request she refused to intentionally misplace Bubba's claim. Although it sounds cruel to fire a young lady for properly doing her job, all turned out well in the end. She eventually married Bubba Jon and now lives in an incredibly large sprawling mansion in Arizona. To pass the time Stella receives and entertains illegal aliens soon after they sneak across the border and holds seminars to show them how to use the chain system to bring in all their relatives. She claimed it was necessary for her to respect her heritage and her illegally immigrated parents. These activities never really bother Bubba Jon because he spends most of his time listening to old Hank Williams records in his custom Airstream trailer out behind the mansion. Tex liked Bubba Jon because, except for his knowledge of minerals, he was an idiot and usually spent all his time at the board meetings just staring at the cleavage of Mary Pintada who mostly sat and tried to look sexy while sucking on her vodka martinis.

To Tex the tough nuts of the group were the next three to arrive. They always seemed to arrive together even though they supposedly hated each other. Tex could never understand this because to him all those middle easterners were all the same and figured if they would all just get together and plant some damn trees, seed their deserts with grass, build a few golf courses, some Wal-Marts and some Home Depot's, then they would all be happy as pigs in shit. But, concluded Tex, no matter how many you kill and how much money you give them they just keep on killing each other because, odd as it was, they practice the same religion differently and make everybody in the world miserable while they're at it. Just the same, as Tex always says, *"Hell, man, their damn money's good so I don't give a rat's ass what kinda horse they rode in on."* But they weren't riding horses when they strolled in wearing their flowing white silk robes and strange headgear. What they wore on their heads always perplexed Tex because it looked like something you'd wear after a shower and too damn hot for the desert. Hell, didn't even call them hats and he couldn't even pronounce what they did call the damn things. At a previous board meeting Tex tried to make them a gift of high priced broad brimmed Texas Stetsons. They nodded their heads in appreciation and on their way out of the building they dumped the hats in the trash. Ever since that time Tex would always wonder which one of the three middle easterners he was going to shoot first when the opportunity finally arose. He never could learn to say their names so he referred to them as the Marx Brothers.

Following the entry of the Marx Brothers, Tex watched as the rest of the business ball and chain gang arrived. It included two lawyers who were always so busy making money that they never actually practiced law, two surgeons who were so busy making money that they never saw any patients, a young entrepreneur who made a billion dollars selling made in America pens and paperclips to the US federal government that were actually made in China, and a fat lady called Mama Kate who somehow turned a recipe for bread pudding into a popular TV show and an all things kitchen utensil and cooking empire.

The group quietly circled the table and found their reserved seats. Mary Pintada sat gracefully and reached directly for her martini while Bubba Jon Jones watched with delight, fantasying over her wet lips as they came away from the glass. He flopped into his chair and smiled widely when Mary gave him a cursory nod. Then there came the Middle Eastern Marx Brothers who hated each other but didn't hate each other as much as they hated what they considered those dumb-ass Americans. Americans, they thought were only good for making money and movies and bad music and wars. To them war was spelled M-O-N-E-Y because they could get America to fight in their countries and then pay massive amounts of money for the privilege of getting American men and the middle eastern masses of the unwashed eliminated. Hence they hated the American Tex the Big Bopper but they loved the way he made them money. So their flowing silk sheets drifted to their high back soft leather chairs where they intended to sit and not pay any attention to anything anyone would say except how much money they were making.

Then sat the doctors and lawyers and the rich pencil paperclip punk from Boston which filled all the remaining seats except one. Everyone knew whose seat that was and it wasn't the big chair at the end of the table reserved for Tex. It was the empty seat with the matching serving set of Qing Dynasty red porcelain.

The two small cups and small container of rice wine was valued at over $15,000,000... each. As for the rice wine, who knows? Finally the door was opened and in shuffled two very lovely Oriental girls who quickly went to the empty chair. One proceeded to wipe the chair on all sides while the other poured the rice wine into the two cups. She then took one of the cups and set it on a small silk napkin in front of Tex's chair as a matter of respect for their host. Once the girls had finished they immediately exited the room and in walked the Honorable Fu Phuc Yu, the man many in the business of international finance often considered to be the single wealthiest person in the world.

Fu Phuc Yu began his climb to financial wealth as a boy in Hong Kong where he became well known as the *kill boy*. For the right amount of money Fu Phuc Yu would kill just about anybody and back in those days business was pretty damn good. Eventually Fu Phuc Yu branched out into real estate and it is well known that due to a severe lack of availability, Hong Kong has the most expensive real estate on the planet. He did very well in that field because he had a very persuasive buyer's pitch. He would say, *"Sell me your house or I will kill all of your relatives."* It didn't take long for people to discover that he meant business and using this method of persuasion, Fu Phuc Yu not only purchased real estate at a very good price, but also manufacturing corporations, shipping lines, a Levi's factory, and a panda pet zoo. All before he decided to branch out and begin investing in America which is when he met Tex. His sales pitch however didn't work well with Tex who immediately pulled out a Smith & Wesson six gun and shoved it in his face. They have been good friends ever since.

"Good. Now that we're all here I can get this here rodeo goin'," said Tex the Big Bopper. "Y'all know I ain't one to fiddle around with a bunch of bullshit at meetins. Got too much shit to do and ain't got no time to be pissin' around up here in office land.

One of the Arabs squirmed a little in his seat and tried to inconspicuously slide his hand down to scratch his ass.

"What's the problem there, Ahab? Your Speedo runnin' up yer ass. Iffin' you wanna step out and fix it we can all wait. Hell man, ain't no shame. We all got ass cracks and know what that's like." Obviously Tex was not known for his etiquette.

"You're wearing a Speedo?" asked the surprised fat lady Mama Kate, wishing she could also wear a Speedo.

"In my country the women do not speak unless requested," replied the irritated Arab.

"Humf. Well in my country of California, women talk as much as they damn well please," replied Mary the Congresswoman.

"I ain't so sure that's a good thang," observed Bubba Jon Jones. "I knew a woman once would never shut the hell up and her man finally shot the bitch," he said. "Shot her dead is what he did. In fact all her kin was so glad he shut her up that they swore to the judge that she done shot herself. I ain't sure the judge believed all them folks but turns out he knew the woman too and I'm thinkin' he wasn't to grievin' about her loss neither. Besides, her husband was the judge's huntin' buddy and that there counts for a lot."

The three middle easterners nodded their heads in approval. "Obviously those people were good Muslims," said one.

"Oh, hell no," said Bubba Jon. "They's just good ol' Pentecostals."

"Can we get on with this meeting?" asked the rich kid from Boston. "I've got to catch a plane back east.

"What, you don't have your own plane?" asked one of the surgeons. "I'll be glad to rent you one of mine."

"I have a plane but I share it with others because that's the correct thing to do."

"Shit kid, what's the point of making all that money if you're not going to take care of number one first?" asked one of the lawyers.

"I have learned to share my wealth. That's how it works where I come from. It's the proper thing to do. Just ask Senator Elizabeth Warren, she'll tell you. She'll tell you that your business isn't your business, it belongs to the people. That's what she'll tell you. That the people built your business."

"Warren! That bitch wouldn't know anything about business. Hell son, that bitch wouldn't know good business if it crawled up her ass," said Tex.

"Oh, okay," said one of the other lawyers. "So you rip off the government of millions so you can share it with other people? Don't you realize that the government's money is the people's money?"

"Exactly," said the Boston kid.

"So why take the people's money in the first place if you're going to, uh… *share* it with them?"

"Yeah, and those folks you're sharing with… bet they're not exactly on food stamps. Not if they're jet setters flying around the country, uh… in *your jet*. Son, I don't know if you're stupid or just plain, um… stupid."

"I'll have you know I have a degree from Harvard."

"Oh, well then, that explains everything," injected one of the surgeons. "Learned all that hearts and flowers crap while you were getting ripped off by Harvard, did you?"

"I have no time for this. I'm leaving," declared Fu Phuc Yu as he began to rise from his chair.

"Now just hold yer horses there super chink. We ain't even begun this soiree yet so sit yerself down and listen up cause I got some bad news and I got some good news but to put it in financial lingo, the good news will fix the bad news. Ya got me?"

Fu Phuc Yu sat back in his seat and listened carefully as Tex the Big Bopper continued. The others nodded their heads in concurrence even though they hadn't a clue what he was talking about. That is all but Mary Pintada who was more interested in her martini.

"Okay folks, so here's how this here round up is gonna play out. Are ya listenin'?"

They all stared at Tex leaving him to think he had their attention with the exception of Mary Pintada of course who, as far as he was concerned, didn't matter anyway.

"You all know what we do here, right?" asked Tex.

"Yeah, we make money," answered Bubba Jon Jones.

"I mean besides that, dumb ass," barked Text.

"Oil and shale and timber and some railroad stuff and a refinery, uh... or two. Um... or is it three?" said one of the lawyers.

"Well, hell son, don't you read them quarterly and annual reports we put out all the time?" asked Text.

"Hell no, I'm a lawyer. I don't read."

"Yep, I figgered as much," replied Text. "Okay folks, here's the scoop. Some of the states is givin' us a hard time about our shalin' operations. It's a political kinda thing all wrapped in the tree huggin' climate changin' shit that all them yuppie fuckers is teachin' our children in school. And they're up our asses about our pipelines even though without them thar pipelines they'd all be burnin' candles and riding horse and buggies. So until Mary here can get some shit happinin' in Washington, our shalin' operation is likely to be only breakin' even. We can also get all that shit fixed as soon as all them there Progressive Democrats and Commies like that Warren bitch quit fuckin' around with the people's ability to make money, but it might take a little while cause Mary there is a little slow on the uptake. No matter. But now here again is another little problem. It seems them damn ragheads over the pond there – no offense there Marx Brothers – well they're sayin' they're gonna start messin' with the oil prices so's to mess up our market place and those Japs and China dudes and crazy Ruskies is talking the same shit, not to mention them fuckin' idiots down yonder in

Venezuela who are so busy stealin' from and starving all their own people that they's goin' outta binness. You know, same old story, we got it and they want it even though they got it but don't know what to do with it. You'd think all those folks would jus' realize how easy it is to jus' do the shit right and rake in the cash. Hell, ain't no big secret."

Tex took a pause and gulped down his honorary rice wine. "Goddamn there Fu. You little people actually drink this shit everyday?" he said while holding back his choking and desire to spit it out. He then hit the button on the intercom in front of his chair.

"Yes Mister Tex," came the perfect lovely soft voice of a woman.

"Honey would you bring me in a shot or two of rye whiskey quick smart?" asked Text.

"Yes Mister Tex."

No sooner had the voice gone away that the door opened and in came the former Miss Texas with a small bottle of Texas Rye Whisky, a glass, and a beer chaser. All the men in the room laser focused on her incredible ass as she glided through the room. That is all except Bubba Jon who focused on her tits.

"Thank ya toots," said Tex just before he gulped down the entire glass of whiskey. "Ahhh… ain't she a cutie? She was Miss Texas ya know. Woulda been Miss America if she met me first," he stated then continued, "Sorry there Fu but I'm afraid I just caint hannel none a that there China juice." He set the whiskey glass down on the table, gulped down the chaser, and continued. "Well all this crap that's affectin' our binness is puttin' my own Speedo in a bunch, if ya know what I mean. Now we all done gone through this kina crap afore so it ain't quite the end of the world, that is unless you Chinamen or Ahabs decide to blow up the world, which brings me to the good news. It seems all them crazy people out there who are so eager to blow up the world can't do it unless they have the right stuff. And that ladies and gentlemen is the stuff we are going to get 'em."

"Oh no!" objected the rich punk from Boston.

"Son, ya gotta let me finish what I'm sayin' before you start sayin' no and objectin' to what I'm sayin'. Hell, I ain't sayin' we're gonna help blow up the world. I'm juss sayin' we're gonna dig up the shit that makes it possible to blow up the world. Kinda like sellin' tobacco or booze. Ain't my no never mind what the hell they do with the shit after they buy it."

"I expect you're talking about uranium?" asked one of the surgeons.

"Linoleum?" said Mary after finishing off her second martini.

"No, uranium," repeated the surgeon.

"Oh, aluminum," said Mary.

"Uranium, you stupid woman," said one of the middle easterners.

"I'm not stupid, I'm a Congresswoman from San Francisco," she answered. "That's in California. Did you know that's in California because San Francisco is in California."

"Exactly," said Bubba Jon Jones. "Explains a lot."

"So, we're talking about uranium," said one of the surgeons.

"You got it," answered Tex. "But I'm talkin' about the good kind of uranium. You know, like there's good cholesterol and bad cholesterol? At least that's what all you doctors are tellin' us so's we buy all that medicine shit that kills *all* the cholesterol, even the good stuff that we *need*. Personally, I think that's a load of crap. I took that stuff once and it put my pecker right outta binness. And we all know all you doctors own all them comp'nies that's makin' and sellin' that shit. Hell man, you folks are killin' more people while your killin' cholesterol than any a that uranium shit."

The doctors looked at each other and shyly nodded their heads, admitting guilt.

"But you're talking about uranium. You can't know what people will do with it once we sell it," said the concerned young billionaire from Boston. "There's no such thing as good and bad uranium is there?"

"Sure there is," said one of the doctors. "I make a lot of money with uranium in hospitals."

"Son, I ain't talkin' about blowin' up the world," said Tex. "Although blowin' up Harvard might be a good idea."

"Then what exactly are you talking about?" asked the Boston Billionaire.

"I'm talkin' about puttin' a cool hundred million a year in your bank account," said Tex.

"Oh. Oh... Okay. That works," replied the Boston billionaire.

"I happen to know there's uranium deposits all over the world," said Bubba Jon Jones the former prospector. "So how you gonna make it more valuable than it already is? And that stuff ain't cheap anyway so your gonna have ta corner the market. Hmm, I see. Yep, you corner the market and that stuff'll be more valuable than blueberry hotcakes at a church fund raiser."

"Yeah, I like blueberry hotcakes," said one of the lawyers.

"What are blueberry hotcakes," asked one of the middle eastern Marx Brothers.

"Yeah, and that stuff is highly regulated by the government. You have to be licensed to just look at it, much less dig it up and process it," said one of the lawyers.

"Blueberry hotcakes are regulated now? I didn't know that," said Congresswoman Mary. "Can I have another martini?"

"Hell ain't nothin' impossible, son," replied Tex. "If that Hillary Clinton bitch could skirt the law all day and get away with it, and she ain't the brightest candle on the cake, then how damn tough can it be. Besides, who says we gotta run the operation in this country anyhow? Hell, we can do it anywhere. You know, like the CIA and General Electric and guys like that. I don't know about you folks but there sure ain't never been no national boundary lines where my money comes and goes. Ya got me?"

He looked around the room and saw agreement, then continued, "Now listen here cause here's the good part. You remember how we developed a satellite that can look down into the earth and find oil deposits?"

They all shook their heads no.

"Gaul damn it, you know you folks really should read those reports some times. I mean you're not just board members, you're the principal investors in this here enterprise," said Tex, shaking his head in disbelief. "Well okay then, just listen up here. It seems we got this satellite that looks down into the earth and can find oil deposits and we also have this kid who works for us who's some kinda genius or sompin'. One of them millenniums or sompin'. Hell, this here kid is so damn good I even farm him out sometimes. Well this here kid has tweaked our satellite so it don't only find oil but it can also find that uranium shit."

"That doesn't mean we can just hop into any old country and dig it up," said one of the lawyers. "There are international considerations and laws and shipping regulations and…"

"All that stuff don't mean nothin'. Not after what we found," grumbled Tex. He tipped his hat up and said, "Ya know you damn lawyers are always making things so gaul damn complicated. Juss shut the hell up and listen."

"I can handle the shipping," said Fu Phuc Yu.

"And my firm can manage and get around all the international laws," entered the other lawyer.

"I'll deal with the marketing," said the billionaire from Boston.

"Hey kid, I thought all you did was sell pens and paperclips to the government," said Bubba Jon.

"Um... I sold the Chesapeake Bay Bridge once. That's how I paid my way through Harvard and um... got my first Ferrari," replied the Boston billionaire. "You should have seen it. It looked just like Magnum's."

"Share that with your poor neighbors do ya kid?" said a sarcastic Tex.

"As a matter of fact I did just that. Um... but they wrecked it."

"There's a lesson to learn there kid," replied Tex.

"I think I handled that deal. The bridge I mean. Not the car," said one of the lawyers. "Oh no, wait, my mistake. That was the Brooklyn Bridge," he laughed. "Sold it to some government guy from India who actually used American aid money for the purchase. Twenty million bucks. Heard he was killed by some other guy because he didn't want to split the profits from the resale."

"Hmm... sounds familiar," mumbled Fu Phuc Yu.

"You said not after what we found?" said the fat bread pudding lady Mama Kate. "Just what have we found?"

"Can I have another martini?" said Mary.

"Ha ha!" laughed Tex as he leaned towards the group over the table. "Baby cakes," he said. "we, the Texas Yellow Rose Corporation, done found the Mother Load cause I'm goin' to cause such a commotion in the uranium market that even that there Russian Putin pussy won't be able to get his hands on any."

"But how will you do that?" inquired Mary, surprising everyone else who thought she wasn't listening. "Can I please have another martini… with three olives?"

A frustrated Tex hit the intercom. "Darlin, will you bring in a bunch of damn martinis for Mary afore she drops on the floor from confusion… with three olives. And ya better bring me another bottle of rye, I think I'm gonna need it pretty soon."

"Yes Mister Tex."

In came the lovely Miss Texas with a tray full of martinis, all with three olives and a bottle of Texas Rye Whiskey.

"Thank you dear," said Mary as she snatched one of them before it reached the table. "My goodness dear, are those boobs of yours the real thing or have you been modified?" she asked Miss Texas.

"Now Mary we ain't here to talk about my secretary's tits. I believe you were originally interested in how we were going to corner the uranium market."

"Aluminum?" said Mary after a refreshing sip of her fourth martini.

"Uranium. Uranium. URANIUM! IT IS URANIUM YOU STUPID INFIDEL WHORE!" yelled one of the Marx Brother Middle Easterners.

"I'm not a whore. That was a fraternity party thirty-five years ago. I told you, I'm a…"

"Stupid infidel woman. Now shut up or I will personally cut off your head."

"Why would you do that?" asked a perplexed Mary.

The Middle Easterner reached for the jewel encrusted gold and silver dagger in his belt but was halted by another who said, "Not now, brother. You must wait until she visits your country and then do it on Al Jazeera TV so you may be respected and known as Mohamed's great messenger."

"How the hell did that woman get so rich?" asked one of the doctors.

"She married a wealthy tuna king,' replied a lawyer.

"Fish? Fish have a king?" said Bubba Jon.

"After you put them in a can they do, dumb ass," said Tex.

"I want to kill that stupid whore," said the Arab.

"Now don't get yer Speedo in an uproar there, Ahab," said Tex. "The lady is stinkin' rich and one of our major investors so she's got a right to be stupid if she wants to. That's the American way and her California prerogative. I don't know why, it just is and somehow it's legal, especially in San Francisco. Now, let's get back to cornering the market on uranium?"

"Aluminum?"

"Uranium."

"Oh, linoleum."

"Just shut the hell up, Mary," said Tex.

"I'm going to cut off her head."

"I just might help you," said Tex. "But not now. Now we talk about cornering the market. That's real simple. We start a rumor that some damn terrorist dudes, probably from your neck of the woods, um or should I say *sand*, in the Middle East, has somehow tainted the world's current supply of uranium in order to cause some kind of chaos or power outage or somethin'. Now, we's all in the oil binness so's we all know how ta control the price of product with rumors and speculation. Ya want the price of oil to go up why then ya juss tell the world that there ain't enough to go around. You know, like they do with sugar and coffee and bacon and such. Ain't nobody knows the difference or that you juss want a new gold plated Lamborghini or a new yacht or villa some place. Ain't no real magic to it. Juss a matter of plantin' the right bullshit in the right place so's it makes its way to those dummies at the New York Times and the Wall Street Journal and them idiots at CNN and NBC."

"Did I ask for two olives or three… or four?"

"Jesus Christ, Mary."

"I'm listening. I'm listening. You were talking about shorting the market on linoleum, um, but I'm not sure how many olives…"

"Three olives, three. Now shut the hell up Mary," said Tex.

"So, there's enough uranium on this island to supply the entire world?" asked Fu Phuc Yu.

"According to the satellite and my genius tech head, yes," replied Tex.

"But who says we can take it?" asked one of the Doctors.

"Nobody, that's the beauty of it. This island don't belong to nobody so's we juss gonna go take it and make it our own damn country."

"You Anglos are always taking other peoples countries," said one of the Middle Eastern Marx Brothers.

"Nah, not always," smiled Tex. "Juss when there's a pot a gold to go with it."

"Are you sure it was three olives?" asked Mary.

Chapter 3

The Mother Load!

In a large dimly lit room deep in the bowels of the NASA Johnson Space Center in Houston three US government Presidential cabinet level individuals along with Vice President Howard Montgomery Hoover Bozer stood impatiently around the desk of a nervous young man sitting in front of a hodgepodge of computer consoles. The young man, intimidated by their presence, stared directly at a computer screen and tried to pretend and in fact wished they weren't even there or that he wasn't there. The young man's name was Roger, known in his home neighborhood since his employ at NASA as *Roger the Rocket Man,* even though he had nothing to do with rockets. The moniker, however, was helpful in putting off all those bullies that picked on him as he grew up and would be picking on him still because he lived in his mother's basement. To reinforce the popular name Roger wore a big NASA patch on all of his outerwear along with a neat official looking baseball hat and nifty teardrop shades like the ones that astronauts wear. It was like a big sign that said *Don't Fuck With Me Because I'm Roger the Rocket Man of NASA* and it let him walk a little taller. He didn't tell anyone that he had purchased the patches and hat at the souvenir shop at the NASA visitors' center and the glasses at a local CVS Pharmacy.

Roger was considered one of the finest brains at NASA but no one would ever tell him that because they thought he was too young to appreciate it and they also didn't want him to take their jobs. As a result, the young computer technician was relegated to a lone position where he monitored and controlled all the secret NASA shit up in space that no one was supposed to know about which basically consisted of only a single satellite. This in turn, rather than giving him extreme confidence, actually gave him a severe insecurity complex. Such is the professional life within a government bureaucracy.

So there he was all alone with the universe at the tip of his fingers, munching cheese nachos and M&Ms, sipping Gatorade and Mountain Dew, and hoping that no one would ever enter his secret abode. Now, however, his private work world was not just being invaded, but was breached by four of the most important heavy-weights in national government. Suddenly Roger the Rocket Man and NASA computer tech was wishing he had taken the job he was offered at Disney World, that of programming and controlling the actions of the creatures in the Country Bear Jamboree.

"If this is true we might have one hell of a problem," said VP Bozer. "If the wrong people get hold of this it could throw off the entire world market for that shit, not to mention the danger of having it end up in the wrong hands. Hell, if that happens it could alter the status of world power."

"And you've got to wonder how anybody has missed this all these years. People have been crawling all over the planet searching out this stuff and here all of a sudden we find the mother load," said Secretary of State, Harvey Hollingsworth Culpepper.

"Right, doesn't make a lot of sense to me either," commented Secretary of Defense, Retired Admiral John Paul Kirkland. "My guess is that Hillary bitch knew about this all along but kept it a secret and hidden in her $15,000 pant suit for some future deal with the Russians so her and her baby raping husband could cash in."

"That all sounds a little portentous, don't you think John?" said the Secretary of the Interior, Retired General Harvey Redcloud. "I mean, just because she rejected you in Little Rock way back in the 80's."

"You mean when I found out she was gay? That's not rejection, that's…"

"Doesn't mean you can always blame everything on her… uh, even though you might be right."

Hearing this, the eyes of the young man sitting at the computer grew wide. His mother was a big fan of Hillary and voted for her. But what would she do if he told her he found out Hillary was gay, especially after years ago when his mother caught his father in bed with man. Maybe she would even ask if he was gay and he would have to tell her the truth because he never lied to his mother - and then his mother would slap the shit out of him and maybe commit suicide.

"Yeah, well. She did that deal with the Russians didn't she?" continued Admiral Kirkland. "She did lots of deals with the Russians."

"Hell, John. Everybody does deals with the Russians. Don't you read the news? Who gives a shit?"

"You mean the fake news?" replied the Admiral. "And all those damn Democrats sure give a shit."

"Yeah, well, it's all those damn Democrats who are doing all those deals with the Russians," replied General Redcloud.

"Shit, go back to the reservation you fuckin' redskin."

"You know where you can go you damn squid."

"Now, now, gentlemen, let's not get into any military service rivalry crap here. We all know what happened between you two in the Army/Navy game way back in the day. Let's put our focus on the problem at hand, shall we?" interrupted Vice President Bozer. "First we confirm the information which is why we're here. Then we make our recommendations to the President. Understood?"

They nodded their heads in agreement.

"Okay son, it's time for show and tell," said VP Bozer. "Show us why we're all here."

"Um... yes sir," said Roger, the nervous satellite technician. "Um, if you will all direct your attention to the big screen on the wall I will call up the view of what our satellite is currently looking at and interpret the readings."

The men turned and moved a little closer to the screen, mainly because they were all old bastards who didn't want to admit they couldn't see a damn thing without their glasses.

Roger continued, "As you know we have satellites that can pretty much see just about anything on the planet. You know, like they can read the time on your watch and all that."

The four men instinctively glanced at their watches and then acknowledged Roger's statement by nodding their heads in agreement with great authority.

"What has happened, gentlemen, is after a recent upgrade by a contractor with the Texas Yellow Rose company in an effort to increase the quality and capability of our sat system we quickly discovered that our little space bird has become a serious bird of prey," said the young man with a smile.

"Cut the comedy shit boy and get to the point," grumbled the Admiral.

"Uh… yes sir," perked up the technician. "You see what happened is we discovered that our newly updated satellite not only looks at what's on the surface but can now look below ground level and detect things like oil and minerals. Now we can kinda do a little of that with other sat programs just like the oil companies but not like this baby."

"And that's how you made this discovery?" asked the Secretary of State.

"Yes sir. And it was one hell of a find, you ask me," replied Roger. He was feeling his high tech oats and was developing a serious craving for a handful of the M&Ms in the bowl sitting by his computer console but just as he was growing courageous enough to do so the big hand of former Naval Academy football fullback Admiral Kirkland reached into the bowl and pulled out the total remaining quantity of the yummy candies.

"We didn't ask you, you little shit, so continue your show," said Admiral Kirkland as he chewed up the M&Ms.

"Yes sir," snapped the young man, thinking to himself that the Admiral was indeed a *real* shit and should switch to decaf or use some of his Quaaludes. "We have permanently positioned our bird over the find. And um… if you watch the big screen I will zoom in and show you the area in question."

On the big screen which currently showed a large portion of the Pacific Ocean, the focus was temporarily lost during the zoom. Eventually a green spot began to grow ever larger in the center of the satellite shot. The four men were all squinting until they finally threw their egos to the wind and pulled out and put on their eye glasses. Soon after the small growing spot covered the entire screen and came into focus. What they were looking at was a small island no more than 15 to 25 square miles in size.

"So you found an island in the Pacific," said Admiral Kirkland. "There must be a million islands in the Pacific. What are we supposed to do, open a Club Med?"

"Admiral, you're a pain in the ass," said VP Bozer. "Let the kid finish will ya?"

The Admiral fell silent and Roger continued. "With these new capabilities we discovered this particular island had a number of natural resources the likes of which may be better collectively than almost anywhere else in the world."

"Resources such as… what?" asked the Secretary of State.

"Oil, gold, diamonds and… uranium. A whole lot of uranium," answered the young man.

"Uranium?" said General Redcloud.

"Yes sir, and not just a little uranium but a whole fuckin' shitpot of uranium - if you will excuse my French."

"And just how much is a whole shitpot, son?" asked VP Bozer.

"Um… you might say it's the mother load, sir. A lot and it's a very heavy compound the likes of which has not been found elsewhere," replied the young man.

"All on this one little island?" asked Secretary Redcloud. "Oil and gold and diamonds? That's a hell of a find by itself. But what's so special about uranium? Got that shit all over the planet," asked General Redcloud. "Even got it back on the reservation. And we have enough problems controlling what already exists. I mean look what that Clinton bitch did and she was supposed to be one of the good guys and keeping the lid on that shit."

"Yeah, *a guy*, you got that shit right," said the Admiral.

"Not like this, sir," injected the young man. "I did some research and discovered this could be the largest single source of uranium of all time."

"So what's the big deal?" asked the Admiral.

"It's the configuration, sir. Not only is it a huge deposit but it's also concentrated or somehow naturally consolidated in one spot where it can easily be harvested by just about anybody in a very short time. Put that together with the other resources discovered and that little island could be the most valuable 25 square miles on earth."

"How do you know this?" asked General Redcloud.

"Well it's rather technical, sir. Actually it might be easier for me to show you than explain it technically. Here let me show you exactly where the concentration of uranium is. Watch the big screen. When I task the satellite for a mineral scan and to search for uranium deposits it shows the findings by creating a flashing line around the location and a series of numbers indicating the amount or density. See there? Those equations on the side there? That's the results of the find and that particular find is higher than any other single location on earth."

The young technician had zoomed in on the island and moved the focus about its surface until he came to the mound where Hooky's big egg was buried. He then zoomed in even further to give his guests a better view. "There it is gentlemen. There in the center of the screen. Most all of the uranium is located right in that spot. Um, seems to be about a two hundred foot circle."

The men moved closer to the screen, stared and studied it.

"What the hell is that?" asked the Admiral.

"Not quite sure, sir," replied Roger as he zoomed in further. "It appears to be some sort of totem pole or something."

"What the… Is that a damn mummy standing there?" asked VP Bozer.

"Um… it certainly appears so, sir. And um, it looks a little crusty. I suppose it's been there for quite a while."

"Why the hell would anybody put a mummy on top of a uranium source?" asked VP Bozer.

"Can't say, sir. There's just no accounting for what ancient people or ancient aliens might have done."

"What? Did you say ancient aliens? You mean at one time there were Mexicans on that island?" asked Admiral Kirkland.

"Is everyone in the Navy as stupid as you?" said General Redcloud.

"Yep, that certainly is a mystery," continued the young man. "But that's not the only mystery. Like what… um…"

"What what, son? Continue," said VP Bozer.

"And well, um… that island doesn't even exist."

"What the hell you mean it doesn't exist?" asked Admiral Kirkland. "We're standing right here looking right at it. This supposed to be some kind of Ghost Island or something. I've heard that sort of scuttlebutt when I was at sea. I remember once when there was a…"

"Hell, Kirkland, you're always out to sea. Damn psycho squid sonofabitch," interrupted General Redcloud. "Let the kid finish."

"Is this some sort of a candid camera punk thing or what?" asked the VP. "If it is, I'll have the head of NASA's ass, damn him."

"No sir, it's not a punk thing," said the young computer tech, all the while wishing it were because he truly hated the head of NASA who was the guy who decided to stick him underground at the space center. He was also a political ass kisser who got his position by scamming his way through MIT. "It's just… well, sir, it's not currently listed or charted. I did, however, find a reference to an island at that location in some old Portuguese records and according to those records, back in 1804 the Portuguese gave the island to France in a trade for a piece of land in South America. So I sent an inquiry to the French government regarding the status of the island and all they could tell me is that according to their records the island doesn't exist. And so there you have it gentlemen, according to the French Government who supposedly own this island, it does not exist."

"Well, seems to me somebody needs to go claim this piece of dirt pretty damn quick," said Secretary of State Culpepper.

"Are you saying you want to own it yourself?" asked General Redcloud.

"Hell no. I'm saying our nation needs to grab it before some nut case like that little turd in North Korea gets hold of it. Gold, diamonds, oil, and uranium could put that little psycho peckerwood on a high that might put all of us underground."

"Guess we better set a meet with the President," said VP Bozer. "Meanwhile I would suggest you prepare a small expedition force and be ready to deploy as soon as a decision is made."

"Yes sir. Not a problem," replied Admiral Kirkland. "Consider it done."

"There's something else, sir," said young technician Roger. "On that island that doesn't exist, I think there are people living there. When I was scanning the island I saw what I first thought was a bunch of pigs but when I zoomed in it looked more like people. I think."

"What you mean, you think?" asked VP Bozer.

"Well, they were all kind of squirming around in a pile on the beach. You know, like one of those Debby Does the Dallas Cowboys movies."

They all just stared at the young man and said nothing simply because none of them wanted to admit they had ever seen *Debby Does the Dallas Cowboys*.

Finally General Redcloud cleared his throat and asked, "By the way, son, what's the name of that island?"

"No official name that I could find, sir. Sorry. However, the Portuguese records called it Wass... uh... Wassmoi... *Was si mas io moaki,*" the young tech said slowly.

"Wassi... sisi...," said the Vice President.

"No, it's Wazza... monaliza," said the Admiral.

"Jesus Christ, Admiral, get the shit out of your ears," said former General Redcloud. "The boy said, *Wassamattayu.*"

"No he didn't, you dumb ass redskin. Go bang on your fuckin' tom-tom and quit trying to play with the big boys."

"Oh yeah. Kicked your ass in that Army/Navy game and put you in the hospital didn't I?"

"It was a cheap shot."

"It should have been a gunshot, dipshit."

Chapter 4

Whatchamacallit Island?

Like all government business, be it domestic or international, top secret or just some Senator porking some under aged girl or boy who is not his wife at a so-called conference that's not taking place at a so-called destination resort that's not a destination resort - *there are always leaks*. So of course the news of the discovery of this amazing island soon became a leak crawling around in the Washington swamp until it eventually slithered into the wrong hands or landed on the wrong ears. The President had been briefed then turned around and briefed the Majority Leaders and Minority Leaders of the House of Representatives and the Senate, a very select group, but unfortunately some of them were Democrats who of course went directly to their preferred members of the press and immediately claimed the President was losing his marbles by claiming he had found a magic island full of gold and diamonds and oil. Fortunately they were not told about the uranium. Also in the group was a Republican who disliked the President because while opposing each other in the Presidential Primary, the now President then candidate said that he had funny ears and was too damn short to serve in the White House. As a result the disgruntled short Senator with jumbo ears claimed the President was spouting about some fantasy island full of riches and lied about the island having uranium and that he was a lousy President anyway because fifty years ago he dated a stripper who used to be married to a Russian Democrat.

The leak or rumor about the island became the cocktail conversation of the week all about town and through the echoes of the media, but for the most part it was dismissed as hearsay and political fodder. It was still a fun point of discussion however, especially at embassy get-togethers which were always a favorite of the Washington elite, not to mention a lot of so called friendly influence peddlers known as lobbyists who want to be seen and appear as though they are actually mingling and earning their money, when in fact all they're doing is setting weekend golf dates in Florida. So in this environment no one actually believed there could be so much wealth on such a small island unless it had a golf course, a full service bar that served epicurean munchies during happy hour, and a massage parlor. Naturally they wrote it off as the bullshit rumor of the week.

However, the interest of a few others was peaked to such a degree they believed the rumor and began a desperate effort to find out more information and especially discover just where this mysterious island was located. This proved difficult simply because Hooky's island didn't have a name, at least a name that anyone was aware of and if they did know couldn't pronounce it. And, of course, the only one who knew the actual location was buried in a big dark room sipping Gatorade and munching M&Ms somewhere in the maze of the NASA bureaucracy which no one, not even the head of the agency, knew of his obscure existence.

One resourceful woman however was relentless in her research. She had been so fascinated by the story that she decided to dedicate all of her time and money to find it, but not to gain its wealth. Her goal instead was to save the natives or pigs that were rumored to live there and to prevent the invasion by the outside world that would ruin those lives forever. Her name was Sammy Sinclair, better known as Slammin' Sammy. Slammin' Sammy Sinclair was a social crusader but not just any social crusader. Slammin' Sammy was smart and beautiful and fearless and would never hesitate to get in your face no matter who you were. And Slammin' Sammy also had a black belt in just about every form of martial arts in existence along with an Olympic Gold Medal because her parents were in the Diplomatic Corps and as they traveled all around the world, Sammy would learn whatever form of martial arts was available. Simply put, Slammin' Sammy could really kick ass and in fact was dismissed from a very prestigious university because she kicked the ass of a professor who tried to get in her pants. She then became a professional campaigner for all forms of causes, such as saving the whales, collecting abandoned cars, promoting Canadian French fries called Poutine, and lobbying for a law that requires all members of the US Congress to pass an IQ test. She stuck to that quest for nearly two years until she was finally convinced that Congress would never establish a stupid law that proved it was stupid simply because it was stupid.

So Slammin' Sammy began her research to find the storied island but not through some cursory search on Google. She began real research where she actually had to go somewhere and dig up old documents and believe it or not, read those documents. Her quest began with the maritime histories on record in the United States, especially those recorded by the New England whalers of the late 19th and early 20th centuries. There she discovered the mention of a French island that inspired her to hop on a plane and head to Paris, France, where she dug through all the records she could find pertaining to French activities on Pacific islands. That was where Slammin' Sammy hit paydirt.

It was there she found the records of the island in question and in fact even discovered its name which was *Wassimasiomoaki*. But the catch was, according to French records, the island no longer existed. According to those particular French records the island was completely destroyed by a nuclear bomb test back in 1958. It seemed Slammin' Sammy managed to discover these records because an ambitious French clerk who was in a hurry to celebrate de Gaulle's new Fifth Republic government in 1958 assumed the bomb test had taken place and jumped the gun. She recorded the test as complete and the island as completely gone do to the bomb blast, and she was in such a hurry to go party that she filed the documents in the wrong file. Slammin' Sammy discovering those records was a total fluke because the French had gone out of their way to destroy all traces of the island's history and existence. They did that because according to an international treaty, nuclear testing in the Pacific was ceased soon after the American's test on Bikini Island. Following that time all tests were conducted deep underground and, of course, the French didn't really have any deep ground for testing that wouldn't screw up their picturesque country. They figured two consecutive wars had screwed it up enough and they weren't ready to cause any more grief and destruction, especially since the Americans wouldn't be around again to pay to fix it up.

Another reason for the French to play dumb was that their test on Hooky's island was actually against the rules and in fact the bomb to be tested was so huge that had it gone off it would have rocked everything from Japan to Australia to Hawaii and even Alaska, and probably would have set off a series of earthquakes and tsunamis all around the Pacific Rim. This was typical because the French were noted for always wanting to come in first in all things. In WWI they were the first to send hundreds of thousands of allied soldiers to their death. In WWII they were among the first to surrender. They were the first to kiss face and at one time were famously known as the first to copulate, though with just what species it's not clear. They were the first to invent Champagne and the first to fall dead drunk and barf in the street after consuming it. And like so many other firsts, they wanted to be the first to develop the biggest and most badass atom bomb ever. Thankfully the test was canceled which means they failed. Thankfully they were also not the first to use the big bomb because the French scientists and technicians weren't exactly the smartest guys in the room and as such they seriously overloaded the big bugger with... (you got it)... uranium.

What no one was currently aware of was the problem now exist that the exceptionally big bad ass bomb sits at Hooky's glowing mummified feet and due to a few minutes of rockin' and rollin' in an earthquake, it's now leaking the uranium's radioactivity - and lots of it.

Our social crusader, Slammin' Sammy Sinclair, had a few strange personality quirks that occasionally required attention such as periodic headaches caused by consuming too damn much sugar or beer that sent her into a rage and lead her to pick the nastiest dude in the bar and kick his ass. And then there were her usual responses to rude people and people who called her names like Bull Dog Betty, and a Ronda Rousey wannabe. Responses that sometimes also became a black belt ass kicking. The only one who was willing to deal with these unpredictable quirks was her lady servant in the form of an Italian midget man named Chow Chow. We say man simply because he actually was a man but in reality, if Chow Chow did not dress like a man no one would know he was one. Chow Chow was, let's say, a little limp wristed, and Chow Chow and Slammin' Sammy got along like, well… let's just say they got along quite well, mostly because Slammin' Sammy would never pick on a little person, especially if that little person was Chow Chow, who by the way, could also kick some serious ass as well. This has led a few people to refer to Slammin' Sammy and Chow Chow as… (should we say it?) Batman & Robin… which of course got their ass kicked.

Chow Chow could kick butt because he had to learn at an early age and out of necessity to defend himself. In a country like Italy that is full of hairy macho swinging gonads, growing up as a gay midget wasn't easy. So Chow Chow became extremely proficient with a walking stick and brass knuckles and when he met Slammin' Sammy while riding on the Orient Express his future was set because big Slammin' Sammy and little Chow Chow seemed to be a match made in Heaven, at least to themselves.

So now after only three lucky days of research, Slammin' Sammy and Chow Chow had discovered the location of the object of their quest and she and Chow Chow were on their way to Wassimasiomoaki, or as Chow Chow pronounced it, Whatchamacalit Island. To get there she had gained passage with a singer musician friend named Jimmy who was flying his own Grumman Albatross seaplane to Japan to give a concert. He agreed to let her tag along and drop her off on the island, partly because they were good friends and partly because he didn't want to get his ass kicked. On the way Slammin' Sammy told Jimmy the story of Wassimasiomoaki Island and encouraged him to visit there on his way back to the states. Of course he agreed… because he didn't want to get his ass kicked.

A small man with thick coke bottle glasses stood in the shaded darkness beside an aircraft hanger watching them board Jimmy's plane. When the plane finally rolled across the tarmac, down the ramp and into the water, revved its engines and took flight, the little man pulled out a satellite phone and made a call. When someone answered on the other end he said in Russian, "Сумасшедшая женщина знает, где находится остров, и она ушла." Meaning, *"The crazy woman knows where the island is and she has departed."* He listened for instructions then replied, "Конечно, конечно. Я узнаю, где и где. Я не подведу вас, премьер-министр Путин." Meaning, *"Of course, of course. I will find out where and follow. I will not fail you Prime Minister Putin."* He turned off the phone and shoved it in his jacket pocket, then reached into his other jacket pocket and pulled out a Bit-O-Honey candy bar. When he began to unwrap it he discovered it had begun to melt and had difficulty pulling off the wrapper which eventually began to stick to his fingers so he shook it continuously in an effort to free it from his hand. As he increased shaking the candy it accidently struck his glasses and off they went. You see, Borris Bolufski was a bit of a klutz and as such often found himself stuck in little situations of his own making. This was one such example. When Borris retrieved his thick coke bottle glasses from the tarmac and failed trying to remove the melted candy from the lenses he immediately noticed the right lens had developed a spider web of a crack. He placed the glasses on his face, turned, and walked into a wall. "Дерьмо!" Meaning "Shit!"

So off they went… Batman & Little Robin, headed to somewhere in the middle of the Pacific Ocean where they would hopefully discover a new people and a new culture and things unknown… or just a bunch of pigs.

Mangia il tuo cuore fuori Indiana Jones, thought Chow Chow as he flew into the unknown on Jimmy's Grumman Albatross with a sound system playing *Beach House on the Moon*.

Chapter 5

Paradise Lost

"Oh my! Look at it. Its paradise," exclaimed Slammin' Sammy as she looked out the window of the plane. Jimmy had circled the entire island with as much interest as Slammin' Sammy but mostly to find a safe stretch of water to land his sea plane. He did, however, during his search catch a glance of a pile of writhing bodies on the beach and thought it might be a pile of horny pigs or something.

"Ya ya, datsa gooda place down dere, but I hopa datsa gots some indoor plumbing. I'ma too damn short to be squattin' inna da woods where dey gotsa creepin' anna crawlin' stuff," said Chow Chow.

Slammin' Sammy gazed out over the island where she viewed picturesque coconut trees and lush green tropical forest. And from the top of a mountain flowed a marvelous waterfall that fell at least 800 feet to a beautiful clear blue river below. A river where she thought for a moment she saw small children playing. She then looked at the beautiful white sand beaches and natural rock jetties and what she thought might be a group of pigs rolling around beneath a palm tree. "It's all so wonderful," said Slammin' Sammy. "We absolutely must prevent the rest of the world from discovering this island," she declared. "And I mean I will let no one, absolutely no one invade and spoil this paradise."

"You meana absolutely nobody? Evena Disney?" asked Chow Chow.

"That might be a tough thing to do," entered Jimmy as he banked the plane to bring it around for a landing on the smooth water of a large lagoon that led to the shore of the ocean. "I mean, just look at it. It'd be a really great place for a Margaritaville resort and casino."

"Now, Jimmy, I love you but if you want to live long enough to land this plane then I suggest you put that shit out of your head."

"Yes ma'am."

Hours later Slammin' Sammy and Chow Chow could feel them watching. They felt them watching when they disembarked from Jimmy's plane and they felt them watching when they dragged all their gear onto the beach, and Chow Chow especially felt them watching when he went and pissed against a tree. But... with all the watching, both Slammin' Sammy and Chow Chow never saw them. "Like children," said Slammin' Sammy. "They're like frightened little children afraid to come out and meet us. How cute."

"I'ma no thinka so cute," disagreed Chow Chow. "I'ma thinka they gonna come out when they gonna kill my little ass."

"Oh no," said Slammin' Sammy. "No such thing could ever happen in such a beautiful place as this. It is indeed a *paradise lost* and we're here to make sure it stays that way."

"How you gonna do dat? You gonna make it invisible or put up a buncha big billboards datsa gonna say 'KEEPA YO ASS OFFA DIS ISLAND OR ELSE'?"

"Or else what?" asked Slammin' Sammy.

"I'ma don' know. Maybe throw rocksa or deada fish or somethin'. Maybe tell everybody thata dissa island is fulla disease and um… bad food. Nothin' worse thana bad food isa what my mamma alwaysa says."

Slammin' Sammy and Chow Chow sat under a coconut tree on the beach for the rest of the day waiting and hoping that some islanders would come to meet them. By nightfall no islanders appeared and so the two intrepid travelers just stretched out. After hours of listening to the breeze as it tossed and swayed the tall palms and the melodic sound of the breaking surf they fell off into a deep sleep.

The morning sun stretched widely over the ocean and as it rose it shot a ray of light across Chow Chow's face causing him to turn to one side. The streak of sun seemed to follow his face and though he continued to keep his eyes closed, his mind slowly began to focus on his surroundings. The sounds and smells of the island and the sea began to sneak into his consciousness until such a time that he remembered where he was. His eyes still closed, he perked his awareness until suddenly he heard what he thought to be whispering. *Whispering?* thought Chow Chow. *Whispering comes from people. People? What people?* wondered Chow Chow who then slowly opened his eyes and squinted through the light, looked from side to side, and discovered they were surrounded by Whatchamacalit natives. "Hooooly'a shit!" exclaimed Chow Chow. "Sammy! Sammy, wake up. We gotta soma company, girl." When he looked to Slammin' Sammy he discovered she was already awake and standing and quite frankly wasn't sure if she was going to make friends or start kicking ass.

They were surrounded by every existing islander, all 68 of them, tall and small, big and little, dark and not so dark, and even a few near blondes, and each and every one of them was buck-ass naked and smiling, and from what Chow Chow could see, some of the island's men had quite a lot to smile about as did many of the young women. Quite simply Chow Chow wished he had the same reason to smile because he wasn't just short in elevation only. He looked to Sammy to find her smiling with open arms and absolutely no degree of shock at the sight of 68 attractive buck-ass naked people who, like fish who don't know they're wet, didn't seem to know or care that they were naked.

For the longest moment everyone, including Sammy and Chow Chow, simply stared and said nothing. Then to Chow Chow's complete surprise Sammy removed her clothes, opened her arms and walked into the crowd as if to say, *I am one of you* (even though I am ten inches taller and have a really hot body with big tits and a nice ass). As they all began to surround her with curiosity, especially a few of the men who obviously seemed to really like what they saw, she turned to Chow Chow and said, "Well Chow Chow, you know what they say, '*when in Rome*' my friend."

Chow Chow knew exactly what she meant. His first thought was remembering that he never liked Rome and as soon as he was able and old enough he left there for points unknown. The other thought that crossed his mind was, *are these people really ready to see a buck-ass naked midget with limited jun*k *between his legs?*

Chapter 6

Texas Yellow Rose Screw Up

"NASA! NASA!" yelled Tex the Big Bopper. "What the fuck you mean NASA? How the hell did NASA find out?" He rose from his big leather chair behind his hand carved mesquite wood desk and darted across the room to Alvin, the very frightened young computer tech. "You said you invented that shit. You said we were the only ones on the planet that had that satellite shit. You said we were the only ones on the planet who knew about this shit! Well! Let's have it, son. What the hell happened? Did you steal it from NASA or what? Everybody and their fuckin' uncle know about our island now. I wanna know how damn it, how!"

"Um… no sir. Of course not."

"Of course not what?"

"Of course I didn't steal it," replied the very nervous Alvin.

"Well then what the hell, son? How come they all know? How come my damn island is now public knowledge? You got any good God dang idea what that does to my plans and my time schedule?" he yelled while pointing his missing finger hand at the young man. "Now I gotta go find me some good ol' boys and rush 'em out to take that there little damn island before anybody else does. And I can't use my boys from the ranch cause it's round up time and they all gonna be busy bringin' in my 3000 longhorns." He paused, then said, "Well, don't jus' sit there boy. Say sompin'."

The young tech head swallowed nervously as he watched Tex rant and rave, come across the room, bend over, and stop a mere foot from his nose, then said only to Tex, "Umm…"

"Um? What the fuck ya mean 'um?' I ain't payin' you for no 'um' answers. I want some gaul darn words," demanded Tex as he reached for his Smith & Wesson six-shooter.

The young millennial tech head Alvin jerked up in his chair and backed his head away from Tex's six shooter. When he did two packs of bubble gum and a Power Bar fell out of his multi-pocketed tech vest. Tex stared at the items when they landed on the floor beside him. "Holy shit, boy. Ain't no wonder you can't open your damn mouth if you're always eatin' that shit. He jammed his gun back into its holster and walked to the bar where he poured a full glass of pure Texas Rye Whiskey then turned and handed it to his computer tech. "Drink it, boy," he ordered. "It'll clear all them computer 1's and 0's and shit off your brain and then maybe you can talk. Might even help you make some sense in what you're sayin'. And you really should stop eatin' that shit and eat some good ol' Texas steak. Yep, a good ol' one pound t-bone will surely cure what ails ya be it brain or body."

The nervous young man carefully accepted the glass of rye whiskey and stared at it. He wasn't quite sure how he should drink it. Should he take it in sips or small gulps or just down it all at once like the cowboys do in the movies? Alvin had always had his head in a computer for most of his life and never ventured to try any spirits. The strongest thing he ever drank was a cup of Listerine mouthwash his religious purist grandmother made him take after he ate an anchovy pizza and she was offended by his breath. He drank it and she told him afterwards that he wasn't supposed to swallow it but just swish it around and spit it out. He swallowed it and hated it. To this day he has always avoided anything that even comes close to looking like Listerine. And this rye whiskey looked a lot like Listerine. The young millennial does however still like anchovies.

"Well don't just stare at it, boy. It ain't no urine test it's jus' good ol' Texas Rye Whiskey. Damn good shit too if I say so myself cause I make it on my own ranch and sample every damn batch for high quality effect and if a batch don't measure up why then I jus' dump it same as I do with my employees that don't tow the line."

The measuring up and towing the line part of Tex's statement struck home because the young man was about to inform Tex that he had screwed up big time. So hearing those fateful words and not knowing if getting dumped included an episode with the Smith & Wesson six-shooter, the boy rose the glass of rye whiskey to his lips and gulped it down in its entirety. As he did and while he attempted to recover from the shock, Tex once again pulled out his pistol and strolled around the office while spinning the cylinder and humming the melody of *The Yellow Rose of Texas.*

Finally, no longer hearing the young man gasp for breath he turned and stood and looked down on him, all the while continuing to fondle his Smith & Wesson. "Ya know my daddy always said the only good gun was a Sam Colt .45 but then my daddy wasn't always right. Example bein' he only made about 200 million dollars in the oil binness as opposed to me. Ya see, in half the time I done made over 200 billion for myself and a buncha other folks... includin' you, boy. So when I say I'm a little prejudiced towards a Smith & Wesson, well then I expect to be heard. And when I say I don't tolerate no failure in my binness then that's exactly what the hell I mean," he said, shaking the gun at the young man. "Now spit it out there, boy. Who the fuck leaked our technology and the information about that thar little island?"

"Uh... the President," the young man said nervously.

"The President? The President of what?"

"Of the United States."

"The President of the United States? That damn pretzel neck idiot! Hell, he couldn't leak in a urinal much less..." He paused and looked down at the young man with serious intent. "Are you pullin' my peter, son? You want me to pop you in the head with this here shooter?"

"No sir."

"Than just what the hell you talkin' about?"

"NASA, sir. Like I said before. He got it from NASA."

"Well how the fuck did them space monkeys get hold of it?"

"Um… with their satellite, sir."

"But you said ain't nobody got that thing except us. And I done told our people that. And I done told everybody that you're the very best there is anywhere in the whole damn world at what you do. But now you're tellin' me that some gubment space cadet done outdid my very best man at his own game?"

"No sir."

Tex stared for a very long silent moment directly into the eyes of his young tech head until he finally spoke, "Son, my life is all about numbers and understanding people and though you might think that's a difficult thing, for me it really ain't difficult at all, but… I gotta tell ya, yer the most confusing sumbitch I ever exchanged words with cause I don't understand a fuckin' thing you're sayin'. Now boy, in my world a man says what he means and means what he says. So let's us give it one more try, Okay? Now, how'd them damn space monkeys down yonder in Florida get hold of a satellite that can do what we can do?"

Alvin's brain went into high gear as he thought through the many possible ways he could answer the question without getting shot by Tex's preferred Smith & Wesson. Then it came to him like a lightning strike and without thinking it through he said, "*You* gave it to them, sir."

"What? I did what? I gave what?" exploded Tex. "What the hell, son, I ain't gave no shit to no space men ever. What the hell you talkin' about?"

"You told me yourself, sir. You called me up here to this very office and I sat in this very chair and you said you made a deal with NASA for my services to help improve their satellite system. You said we would make a shit bucket full of money doing what those over educated dick heads couldn't and that's why they always bid everything out to folks like us. You said, and I quote, '*Son, I want you to pop on down there and jack up their damn satellite shit and then get on home here with that big fat check of gubment money.*' That's exactly what you said so that's exactly what I did. But you also said I only had a week to do it because you had no intension of paying for any of your people to be doing the limbo on the beach with a bunch of drugged out bikini girls when they should be back in Texas doing their job. Um... that's what you said... sir."

"I said that?"

"Yes sir, you said that."

"So what. That still don't explain nothin'"

"Well sir, in order to complete their satellite upgrade within the time constraint you set, I was forced to use my existing programming rather than write new programming. But somehow my programming enhanced their sat system and taught it to do the same things our sat system does." The young tech head knew that excuse was impossible but figured Tex was so technically dumb that he could get away with it. Also, he didn't want Tex to know that he had actually used their original sat programming to upgrade that of NASA so he could go do the limbo on the beach with a bunch of bikini girls.

"So what you're tellin' me is… our basic genius shit which is your genius shit contaminated their genius shit and now their genius shit somehow taught itself to do what our genius shit does."

"Yes sir. Exactly, sir."

"And this is just because I didn't want you to do the limbo on the beach with a bunch of sexy bitches in bikinis?"

"Yes sir."

"Did you do the limbo on the beach with a bunch of bikini girls?"

"No sir."

"Why the hell not. You some kinda gay virgin or somethin'?"

"But you said…"

"Son, when it comes to getting'' a little now and then, whatever I say don't mean squat. Hell, boy, that's what makes the world go round. So there was no limbo and bikinis?"

"No sir. I have skinny legs and I don't go out in public in a bathing suit."

"So you're sayin' *I'm the one who fucked up?*" asked Tex as he once again began to fondle his Smith & Wesson six-shooter.

"Oh… um… well… I wouldn't… um… say… um…" The young man looked to his empty glass of Tex's Yellow Rose Texas Rye Whiskey for courage, all the while wishing like hell it was full to the brim and he could gulp it down to dull the upcoming pain, and then asked, "Um… are those real bullets?"

Chapter 7

Who Wants It Anyway?

In Beijing, China, a small group of government officials were meeting to discuss what they thought could become an international crisis if it were not handled swiftly and carefully. After ten minutes of bowing to each other, drinking tea, and each sizing up the other to decide which one he would have to kill to gain control of the country - for future reference of course, just in case - they sat and sternly faced one another trying to look most authoritative while presenting an appearance of childish innocence, also to not give away the fact they were fucking up their area of the empire and stealing millions of Renminbi from the people who would never get it anyway. The idea of knocking each other off was a despicable concept and not preferred by all public officials, but admittedly it was the most expedient way to reach a specified goal because there were just too damn many other people in China willing to knock off other people to climb up the bamboo ladder where they could rule and kill other people. Therefore, assassinations were no big deal in China simply because there were so many Chinese to assassinate. Also, whenever a top official got a case of the ass he would simply assassinate a bunch of people for any number of reasons or excuses. At this time, however, no one in the group had any intentions of assassinating anyone except for the honorable *Chun-mei Fu Quang*.

Chun-mei was an ambitious man simply because of the curse of his name. Chun-mei's parents wanted a girl but the Chinese government had put a limit of how many children each family could have and what gender those children could be and at that time the government decided there were too many women so they declared that only males could be born during that year. It was kind of like America's method of controlling the deer population or protecting the wackanook turtle population even though no one on earth has ever seen a wackanook turtle. Actually, at the time the Chinese were doing long term planning for a massive army and decided they wanted an excess of males to build up their forces, especially after sending a half million of their soldiers to die in the Korean war. Chun-mei's parents were instead determined to produce a female in spite of the great honor of producing a future dead soldier, even if it meant going into hiding after a girl was born. And so when their boy was born his parents put a big bird (the finger) in the eye of their communists party rulers by naming him *Chun-*

mei', meaning *spring plum-blossom (a feminine name)*, *Fu,* meaning *abundant, rich, wealthy,* and *Quang,* meaning *strong, powerful, energetic.* Their logic as well as an assortment of ancient potions and drugs, (as we all wrongfully assume that all Chinese people are just chock full of logic which is why they are so damn good at doing laundry, manipulating their currency for profit, and making fortune cookies), was to create a female offspring. But what they did instead was created a male who talked with a lisp and liked smelling like spring blossoms. It seems their dream girl/boy child turned out to be a little light in the loafers and their hopes of his getting stinking rich and setting them up big time for life in California, was looking less likely each day. What they got instead was a guy who learned to kick ass and fuck people over at every turn because they all thought, due to his name and lisp that he was gay which he wasn't. The only plus of his name was that women trusted him and as a result he got laid a lot without having to threaten death as an option. For Chun-mei, being a badass paid off and as soon as he successfully rose to power to the point where he could assassinate people en masse, he had his parents killed along with 500 others to demonstrate he was a serious administrator. Soon after that half the population in his district moved to Beijing because most of them had made fun of Chun-mei's name and lisp when he was growing up and feared they would be in the next group of 500.

"It is only a small island," offered one member of the council.

"Yes, and in a like manner so is Taiwan. And look at what a pain in the ass that is," said another.

"But it is far away. Is it truly worth the risk of a possible international conflict?" asked another.

"Who gives a shit," entered Chun-mei with a lisp. "The rewards far exceed the risk."

"What risk?" ask a council member.

"What rewards?" asked another.

"The risk. You know. The Americans." said one.

"Americans? What the hell are they going to do?" asked Chun-mei. "All they will do is make speeches and complain and say it doesn't belong to us and anything we do there will constitute a violation of human rights and international law and then they will elect a Democrat and forget all about it."

"But there are no humans on that island. You saw the satellite pictures. There are only a bunch of horny pigs."

"Exactly," replied Chun-mei. "But we must secure the island for ourselves before anyone else does. Have you forgotten that the French claim that it doesn't exist?"

"Why not just build an island out there. We're getting pretty good at that. Nobody owns that part of the ocean so if we build an island out there it will become our ocean for hundreds of miles in all directions." suggested one of the men.

"We could even put a birdcage stadium on it like the one we built for the Olympics." suggested the member who began his career teaching school. "Then we could host international science fairs and ball games."

Chun-mei stared for a moment, wondering why this member was still alive. "It's only 25 square miles. Why would we build another birdcage stadium there anyway?"

"As the great Chairman Mao would say, *'Build it because I say so,'* and we all know our people always need a little *say so* or else they'll just piddle around in those rice paddies all day creating food instead of making shit for Wal-Mart," replied the former school teacher.

"You mean *'Build it and they will come',*" said one of the members.

"That wasn't Mao dumb ass. It was some guy in a corn field in America," said Chun-mei.

"Why not just make a statement and tell the world it is our island and that it's been our island for more than two thousand years," suggested one member. "A sacred island."

"Yes," agreed another. "We can say it is a sacred place and it must not be approached by any foreigners."

There were nods of agreement all around the table with everyone agreeing it would be a lot easier to send out a written statement to the world than actually going and taking over a deserted tropical island.

"And then after a couple more Christmas orders from Wal-Mart we can go there and build a Navy base with a new aircraft carrier and an airstrip and missiles that would enhance our ability to attack those crazy ass

Americans who are always bitching about human rights," said one.

"My thoughts exactly," said Chun-mei. "But we must go now to secure our rights and privileges there, to demonstrate a presence and ownership."

Chun-mei was eager to secure *Whatchamacalit* Island because he had seen the satellite results and the stolen reports from Washington regarding the gold, diamonds, oil, and, most importantly, the uranium. This was information of which he had not shown to the rest of the Chinese State Council simply because he wanted to get to the island and claim it for himself. And to achieve this he was willing to do most anything, starting with the assassination of that stupid ass school teacher. His motivation for this was because once a year he would travel to Hong Kong and while there he was always the guest of a man named Fu Phuc Yu who was considered the richest man in the world. In Chun-mei's mind, Fu Phuc Yu was an arrogant jerk who flaunted his wealth and in fact had no idea at all how much he was worth from one minute to the next because his money was always making more money. Chun-mei was also jealous because Fu Phuc Yu was better at killing people than he was.

Chun-mei's goal was to declare this island a sovereign country, his sovereign country, and get richer than Fu Phuc Yu had ever dreamt to be. He wanted to have so much money that he wouldn't be able to count it all or know how much money he actually had from one day to the next. And in his new country people could have whatever kind of babies they wanted and their children wouldn't be messed up in the head like he is, and he could kill as many people as he pleased even though he wouldn't need to. And the best part was he could open his very own casino just like the ones in those American movies.

Chapter 8

Gold and Diamonds!

"An island? Gold and diamonds! Are you shitting me? But I thought we cornered the market on gold and diamonds long ago. Oy vey, why do you think everybody in the world wants to kill us," said Israeli Prime Minister Malachi Manheim of Israel into his telephone. "It's because we got that shit by the balls and nobody shines or glitters without first being handled by us Jews. Be it prince or pauper, if you want to strut your stuff with some bling bling then you've got to pay and if we're going to keep them paying then we have to get that island." He concluded the call and placed the phone back in its cradle.

"But grandpa, isn't that unfair?" asked little Betzalel from across the room.

"No grandson, there is no such thing as unfair when it comes to making money. You should always remember that. It is always fair to make money but it is not fair to lose money," said the wise old Malachi.

"Yes, grandfather. I will always remember that," replied the boy.

"You're a stingy old bastard," injected the old man's wife, Samara. Samara had been pissed off at Malachi for the last six years because he would never let her take a vacation trip to Miami to visit her sister because he hated her sister, and also she discovered he had been having an affair with a female member of the Israeli Mossad who had been assigned to protect them from Muslim terrorists. It didn't actually surprise her but it did concern her that there eventually may be an offspring who would end up diluting the inheritance she will get after she bumps him off.

המ לכ. קסעה לע עדוי התא המ. הנקזה הבלכה תא ימתסת וה," ד יוד שאתה.זה את לעשות לא כסף להוציא איך הוא הוא ע Meaning - Oh shut up you crusty old bitch. What do you know about business? All you know is how to spend money, not make money."

"I will make money when they put you in the ground," replied Samara.

"You know nothing of making money and nothing about diplomacy."

"Oh yeah, you think so? Well I ask you this, what about the oil? You always want gold and diamonds, gold and diamonds, gold and diamonds, but what about all that oil and the uranium on that island? I know about that because I listened to your phone call. What about that? What about the oil and uranium?"

"Oil! My god woman, oil? Don't you see if we get into oil we'll have every damn Muslim in the world invading and overrunning this country and not stopping until they have wiped out every last Jew on the planet, and that's a lot of Jews, especially in America. And then the Americans would have to wipe out all the damn Muslims. Those dead Jews are the ones who run all the major corporations and that would start another world war and who knows what will happen after that," said the old man. "And killing all the Muslims? Then who would overpay money for our gold and diamonds? Why just last week my company alone sold five million dollars worth of gold to a rich Muslim Sheikh who wanted to give one of his children a gold plated Jaguar car. You see, it could destroy the market because all those rich Muslims are the ones who buy all that gold and all those diamonds. Oh, and the Indians too. And some Americans."

"And they don't mind buying all that gold from a Jew?" asked Samara.

"Well, what they don't know won't hurt them. Besides, where else will they get it?"

Malachi was revered throughout Israel for three things; he was a hero of the six-day war in 1967, he was extremely good at making money (with gold and diamonds), and he was famous and respected for having an enormous penis (even in his old age). These things eventually led him to become the Prime Minister of Israel.

"And the uranium? Just what would you do with the uranium you stupid old mule?" questioned the old man.

"Don't call me a stupid old mule you stupid old man," replied Samara angrily. "What if we want to build some more nuclear bombs? Have you thought of that? That's what we can do with the uranium."

"We don't need to build bombs. It's too damn expensive. Besides, we get all our bombs free from the Americans. They give them to us because we promise not to use them."

"Oh sure. You have all the answers don't you? And just what do you think is going to happen when the Americans find out that you want that same island with all that gold and diamonds and oil and uranium that they want. What then, smart ass?" asked Samara standing with her hands on her wide elderly hips. "Huh? Tell me. What then?"

"Samara, I sometimes believe that after all these years with me at the head of our government that you would have learned something by now. The Americans are no problem at all. All we have to do is say we are going to claim the island and they will immediately pay us a billion dollars and give us a half dozen new F-35 fighter jets to leave it alone," smiled the old man. "And that's what we will do. There you see, problem solved." he looks to his grandson and shook his finger, "And that my boy is called diplomacy." He then rose and went into another room to take care of business.

After his departure Samara looked to the boy and said, "You see how it works Betzalel? You're grandfather has grown old and stupid but will never admit it. His wife, however, is still vital and wise and has just manipulated him into creating a plan and strategy that not only benefits everyone but will make us rich as well which means I will be able to go visit my sister in Miami. And this should prove to you that Jewish mothers rule the world. Always remember that."

"Yes ma'am. Jewish mothers rule the world. I will always remember."

Chapter 9

The Black Ass Bar

On the coast of Madagascar in a town called Sambava is an old poorly lit and poorly ventilated bar, eatery, and general hang out known as the *Black Ass*. Nobody really knows why or how it came to be named the Black Ass but the rumors were plenty and involved everything from animals to indigenous natives, mostly inspired by the very strange South African founder named Adolf. The most popular rumor had to do with the natives, however, it could never be confirmed because the original owner had long since died soon after he sold the place back in 1968 to an American deserter from the Vietnam War. The speculative rumors about the relationship of Adolf and animals have persisted ever since, especially after it was discovered he was a former post war NAZI in hiding.

The bar is famous for three things being; it never runs out of booze, it has the best looking over-aged waitresses, and it serves the best Foza sy hena-kisoa in all of

Madagascar; a dish that usually consists of stir-fried pork and crab with rice and usually served with the popular drink, *Three Horses Beer*. The Three Horses Beer was necessary to cover up the taste of the pork which was not always pork and had no real name when it wasn't pork.

The current owner known as Crazy Bob had lots of friends who seemed to almost live at the Black Ass primarily because they didn't have anything else to do and everybody there spoke English. In fact the only time they left the place was to get some sleep, get a bath, or get laid, not necessary in that order. Almost all of Crazy Bob's friends were just like Crazy Bob, American Vietnam deserters whose average age was somewhere between 65 and 70. The one exception was a slightly younger Australian named Duffy MacDugal who swears he wasn't a deserter because he deserted before he even arrived in Vietnam and, he claims, it wasn't because he was afraid to fight in the war but because he didn't want to die while he was still a virgin. For some young military men that's important. Before MacDugal was to deploy from Australia to Vietnam he got stoned and caught a ride on a catamaran full of rich equally stoned hippies. Eventually he jumped ship in Madagascar because he was sure that sooner or later the stoners were going to capsize the boat and die. That was in 1972 and Madagascar is where he's been ever since. The question of whether or not MacDugal is still a virgin is kind of up in the air.

Tonight at the Black Ass it was Tuesday and Tuesday at the Black Ass meant that this night would be like any other night with all the over the hill deserters shooting pool, drinking Three Horses Beer, and telling lies about all the combat they were or were not involved in. After five or six bottles of Three Horses Beer they would always start talking about women – mostly American women – mostly American movie star women or maybe some woman they saw in a porno movie in Manakara. But at the moment, after only two Three Horses Beers they were all just joking and trying to not pay attention to Herpie Fisher tell his same bullshit combat story he's been telling for nearly fourty-five years. Once in a while someone would correct Herpie because he would forget something or add something or get some minor fact of his story wrong.

How Herpie got his nickname is pretty much self evident and he didn't really mind it as long as his fellow deserters agreed to keep it to themselves. To achieve this they've also kept a near forty year record of every woman Herpie ever screwed. Partly to keep score and partly to have a list they could refer to so they could avoid getting herpes – or so they said. They actually didn't mind doing that because it was something they could do together and it was things like that which made them a tight knit group, kind of like being in a quilting club. There were seven of them all together in their Black Ass deserter club, eight when you include Crazy Bob, and except for Crazy Bob who was behind the bar laughing, they were all circled around the pool table correcting Herpie who was trying to defend his latest miss remembrance.

It was late and as usual the bar was pretty much empty except for the Black Ass boys and two American FBI guys sitting at a corner table drunk on their asses after only three Three Horses Beers. Unlike American beer, Three Horses Beer was not pasteurized which means it had a pretty good kick. These particular FBI guys enjoying their beer were what the deserters called *searchers* because their job was to search out and find military deserters and bring them back to the states for prosecution. But since the end of the Vietnam War there hasn't been a big demand for searchers. Out of sympathy and self preservation the Black Ass boys decided to help them out by keeping the searchers employed. The Black Ass boys agreed to let the FBI searchers know whenever a deserter died at which time they could hop a plane and zip on out to Sambava, Madagascar, get drunk and get laid and then take the deserter's body home and claim they tracked the guy down and found him dead or that they shot him when he wouldn't surrender. It didn't make any difference to the Black Ass boys because the dead deserter was already dead and he was now going home to his family who had been told all these years by the military that he was a missing POW and as such was a hero. So far the men of the Black Ass have gotten away with the deceased deserter trick five times and at the current rate of dying deserters they figured they were good for at least eight or ten more years. On this occasion the death of their comrade Samson Chillea would make it a half dozen.

Samson was killed by a wandering back-jungle native while he was on a fishing trip in the hills. He was killed with a machete because he wouldn't give the guy his cigarettes. To excuse the mutilated condition of the body the government was going to claim he had been tortured to death by a group of rouge communists who were taken out by SEAL Team 6 on a secret rescue mission in Cambodia. That way the government's long lasting lie was covered up and the SEALs got another feather in their hat and a better budget. The best part of the deal for the Black Ass deserter gang was that while they were still alive the FBI guys would leave them alone and happy. So the FBI agents were now in Sambava getting laid and drinking all the free Three Horses Beer they wanted at the Black Ass. Lately, they had even begun smuggling Three Horses Beer home in the dead deserter's coffins and sharing it with all their friends in the J. Edgar Hoover FBI Headquarters building in Washington. The beer became so popular that it got to where the agents there just couldn't wait for another deserter to drop dead.

Here it was just another Tuesday night and the old boys were now four bottles of Three Horses Beer into the wind and singing *We Gotta Get Out Of This Place* when through the door there appeared a long tall man with rattle snake boots, a broad brimmed Stetson hat, a white goatee, and two missing fingers.

"All right all you losers, I don't like wastin' no time so listen up!" he yelled. "I'm Tex the Big Bopper and you here men are now workin' for me. You got that?"

The Black Ass crew paused and turned and stared at the big tall Texan as though he were some freak trying to moonwalk while doing a very bad Michael Jackson imitation. Finally MacDugal spoke up, "And just who the hell be you, mate?"

"Jus' shut the hell up and listen dude," said Tex as he walked further into the bar. When he did his eyes adjusted to the low light and he could now see the men more clearly. "God damn almighty. You fellas are older'n dirt," he said with surprise, then turned to the small man beside him. "I thought you said these dudes were combat ready. How the fuck am I gonna take my island with a buncha old ladies?"

"Who you calling older than dirt old ladies, buddy?" said a voice from behind the bar.

When Tex turned to see who was talking he discovered Crazy Bob with a double barreled sawed off shotgun pointing right at him. Next to Tex stood his young millennial tech head Alvin, who immediately slid behind him to use the big Texan as a shield against the possible shotgun blast.

"Word is you dudes is a buncha combat vets for hire. But I ain't seein' much here worth hirin'. Hell, looks to me you boys got one foot in the grave already. Hell, some a you old bastards look like you're already dead and might even don't know it."

"This guy's not exactly the prize of the Texas school system is he?" mumbled Corky. The gang around the pool table snickered.

Tex was correct about them being available for hiring but what he didn't know was they usually just hired out for construction work and there hasn't been anything new built in Sambava since some dumb guy from India tried to start a Dairy Queen that went belly up because he couldn't get any real milk to make ice cream which didn't really matter because he didn't know how to make it anyway. Also because his wife thought cows were sacred and eating any part or product of a cow was a terrible thing to do – so she cut him off until he changed his ways. The Dairy Queen is now a Chinese takeout that also sells Indian cuisine. That was eight years ago and the last time the Black Ass boys hired out. Their main source of income now is money from relatives at home who know they're alive and share their government compensation money. Like many of the dead deserters who went home in a box, these guys were considered unclaimed prisoners so their spouses still got benefits which in turn was forwarded to Madagascar.

"You come into my bar to insult my friends. That's a good way to go out the back door feet first," declared Crazy Bob.

"I got a proposal for some good fightin' men but I'm thinkin' I came to the wrong place," said Tex.

"State your piece there cowboy and then get the hell out of my bar," said Crazy Bob.

Before Crazy Bob could react, Tex whipped out his preferred Smith & Wesson, pushed the shotgun aside and put the pistol to Crazy Bob's nose. "I'm Tex the Big

Bopper of Dallas, Texas, home of America's team, the Dallas Cowboys, and big oil and ain't no dipshit in no dive ass bar in some third world shithole of a country gonna threaten and tell me what to do. Now like I said formerly, I don't like wastin' no time and because of the time I ain't got ta waste so's you ol' farts are jus' gonna have ta do. Now everthang's been set, all your gear, guns, and transportation is waitin'. Any questions?"

"Yeah," laughed MacDougal. "Just what the hell are you talking about, mate? And while we're on the subject, just what does it pay because you know we're pretty bad ass and we don't work cheap, especially for some damn roo pokin' fucker from down under the states in that strange place they call... Texas."

"Can I shoot that one?" Tex asked of Crazy Bob.

"No," replied Crazy Bob. "He's Australian and they don't die well unless they're being commanded by a Brit."

"Hey there mate. I'll have you know I can die as good as any man. Especially as good as any yank," objected MacDougal.

"Hundred thousand," said Tex.

"Hundred thousand... each?" asked MacDougal.

"I would really like to shoot that damn Aussie," mumbled Tex. He then exhaled in frustration, "I didn't say *each*. Did I say *each*?" He took a thoughtful pause and figuring half of these guys wouldn't live long enough to collect said "Yeah, okay. A hun'erd thousand each but you buy your own smokes and beer," agreed the compromised Tex.

The millennial tech head Alvin was surprised that Tex agreed so readily. All the way on their trip from Texas the Big Bopper seemed to negotiate everything with everyone, even his own pilots of his own jet where he negotiated a lower per diem. It was embarrassing thought tech head Alvin, because Tex was a billionaire five times over. "It's the deal." Tex would always say. "It's all about the deal, kid. Ya gotta practice the deal or ya ain't gonna be a damn good deal maker. Know what I mean?"

"Now hold on a minute," said Black Ass deserter Corky Ritter. Corky was the smart one of the Black Ass bunch and the quiet type and he could always be depended on to cover everyone's back with an intelligent approach to any problem. "Nobody comes in here and starts throwing around that kind of money for nothing, especially for a bunch of old farts. So cut the crap and fill us in or get the fuck out. And put that damn pee shooter of yours back in the saddle before I take and shove it up your ass." Corky was a former All-American college linebacker for the Florida Gators and also a former Green Beret officer in the 5th Special Forces and even at his current age was quite capable of kicking some big tall Texas ass.

Tex smiled. He was beginning to appreciate the attitude and gumption of this group of old farts and besides, he had done his homework and discovered that prior to their desertion they were accomplished top grade combat experienced soldiers one and all except for that Australian guy. He couldn't find any info on him but decided to let that slide. "Okay partner, here's the deal," said Tex. "There's this here island out there in the middle of the ocean. It's, well, I'll let my little tech guy Alvin here fill ya in." He reached behind and pulled out the millennial tech head kid who smiled shyly then began to speak.

"Um… Hi. Glad to meetcha," he said. 'Um, the island in question is only approximately 20 to 25 square miles. As far as we know it is uninhabited except maybe for a bunch of wild pigs hanging around some old village. But our satellite has indicated that it is loaded with…"

"…coconut trees. And it don't belong to nobody and I want it," Tex interrupted to prevent the kid from giving away the true value of the island. "So's all you dudes gotta do is get on the damn thing, post my flag, and claim it for the Texas Yellow Rose Comp'ny – that's me. You know what I mean, kinda like that Ponce de Leon dude did down there is Florida."

"So what's the big hurry?" asked Corky. "What's so special about this deserted piece of dirt?"

"Well, seems there's some other folks want it juzz like me. So I gotta get it first. That's where you come in. You gotta get there and claim it and hold it."

"What other folks?" asked Crazy Bob.

"Nobody special," answered Tex. "Jus' the U.S. Gubment, and the Jews, and the Russians, and the Chinese, and Koreans, and some crazy tree huggin' bitch called *Slammy* or somthin'. At least that's all my investigators have come up with. But now there ain't nobody there but a buncha little piggies and when you dudes get there you can eat all them pigs you want cause I'm a beef man myself and I ain't real fond of no pig meat and don't want no pigs on my island." Tex paused. "Don't even eat bacon."

"Sounds like quite a crowd," said Corky.

"Gentlemen," said the millennial tech head Alvin, "you should know that this island is a warm climate natural tropical paradise with white beaches, lush forest, abundant wildlife, coconut trees, mountains, and beautiful freshwater falls. Why once you get there you probably won't even want to leave."

Hey, this kid is gittin' the art of the deal, thought Tex.

"Hmm, smells a little hokey to me. Why do you want this place so bad," asked Crazy Bob.

Tex hesitated for a moment then said, "There's somp'n on that island I want real bad."

"And just what the hell would that be, coconuts?" asked Jimmy "T-Bone" Carter. Jimmy was a South Georgia farm boy who didn't speak much except when he had something important to say.

"Um… the remains of… Amelia Earhart," lied Tex.

"And you're going to spend all this money just for a bunch of bones?" asked Corky.

"Well… she was… um, my grandmother."

The Black Ass bar gang looked at each other in silence. After two more Three Horses Beers they agreed that finding the remains of the famous Amelia Earhart was a noble cause and decided for that reason to come out of hiding… and also for a hundred thousand bucks each.

Tex and the millennial tech head kid departed and a few minutes later the FBI guys started to sober up.

"We want to go," mumbled one of the FBI agents before he took a gulp of his Three Horses Beer.

"What?" asked Crazy Bob.

"Us two here, we want to join you on this job," said the FBI agent.

"Why would you want to do that?" asked Herpie.

"Yeah, why would we want them to do that?" asked T-Bone.

"Cause that Tex guy is a liar," replied the other Agent.

"Lying about what?" asked Corky.

"Those bones, there not Amelia Earhart's bones at all. In fact there are no bones… except maybe some pig bones. Everybody in Washington knows about that island. It's full of gold and diamonds and oil and uranium. It's the richest piece of dirt on the planet. That's why everybody wants it and that's why we want to go. We're tired of chasing you pussies all over the planet for a crappy government paycheck."

"So how come nobody owns that little pop of an island?" asked T-Bone.

"Because nobody knew about it until now. And now everybody knows and everybody wants it."

"But who owns it?"

"Nobody. That's the beauty of it. Whoever gets there first gets the prize. So, are we in or what?" asked the FBI agent.

The Black Ass boys all stood dumbfounded for the longest time until Crazy Bob made a crazy suggestion. "So what ya say we go ahead and take that island and then keep it for ourselves. I don't know about you boys but I wouldn't complain about being stupid rich for my few remaining years and then these searchers here drag my old ass back to the States."

They all nodded their heads in agreement. The two FBI agents rose saying, "So we can tag along?"

"Sure," said Corky. "But if anybody inquires, you say you're deserters just like us. Don't want any known feds scaring away the job."

"But what about Samson?" asked Herpie. "He was my best friend. What about Samson?"

"We'll just stick him in the cooler. He's not going anywhere," replied Crazy Bob. "Don't worry, he'll be here when we get back."

"In the cooler! With the Three Horses Beer?" asked MacDougal.

"Sure," said Crazy Bob. "Like I said, he ain't going no place and he sure as hell ain't going to drink all the beer."

"Okay, that works for me," said Herpie.

Chapter 10

The Full Monty!

After only two days on Whatchamacalit Island, Slammin' Sammy and Chow Chow had managed to melt right into the native culture; discovering that the natives were quite welcoming and open to new arrivals. Sammy was now free and happy and buck ass naked mingling with the natives since the first day but Chow Chow didn't give in to the Full Monty concept until the next day when he was coaxed by the island's children who thought Chow Chow was the coolest thing since coconut jelly and the oldest kid they had ever seen. It was also debated whether he was a male or female. He finally stripped down but kept his fanny pack around his waste in such a way that it could prevent his being compared to all those gifted native men. After he did so the children celebrated and danced around singing Chow Chow's name, chanting in their very strange language, *"Chow Chow the old boy. Chow Chow the old boy!"* Still he was paranoid about his ass flapping in the breeze and continued to have concerns about the lack of indoor plumbing. Eventually, however, he did come around to appreciating the benefits, the health and well-being of freewheeling, so to speak, at every turn. Sunshine, fresh air and pissing on any tree or bush whenever the mood arose was fast becoming second nature and, of course, trouble free.

Though Sammy was quite proficient in a number of foreign languages and on occasion caught the hint of a few of those languages while trying to talk with the islanders, she simply had nothing but frustration in understanding them completely, and most of all informing them that the rest of the world was hell bent on coming to ruin their lives. Finally, during the fifth day while sitting with a group of the women making coconut jelly she tried once again to tell them the bad news. As she spoke they all watched, smiled, nodded their heads, giggled, and continued boiling their jelly mix even though they had no idea what she was saying. One girl with a tint of blonde in her hair was watching Sammy carefully while she spoke and neglected what she was doing. Out popped her large wooden spoon from the pot she was stirring and splattered hot jelly on her arm. "Ouch, fuck!" she yelled. "That shit burns!"

Sammy perked up at the girl's use of English and immediately moved and sat by her side. She began treating the girl's minor burns and asked, "Do you understand what I'm saying?"

"Hell yeah," replied the girl.

"You are speaking English."

"What is English?"

"English is the words you were using when you got burned."

"No shit? Is dat what I do? English?"

"Yes," replied Sammy. "Who taught you to speak English?"

"My fuckin' daddy," said the girl.

"He taught you to curse?" asked Sammy.

"What curse?" said the girl.

"Those words you say. Some of them are curse words. Some people think they are very bad. You know *bad*."

"Yes. Bad words? Why bad words? They don't hurt nobody," said the confused girl. "Everybody think they funny words. They think I funny too. You say I bad girl for bad words? Why? I don't know."

"That's not important now. What's important is that we can talk to each other. There are things I must tell your people. Very important things they must know."

"But they already know things. Food, weather, funglu," said the girl. "Nothing else to know."

"Funglu? What is funglu?" asked Sammy.

"Nice Stuff. You wait, you see," replied the girl.

"What is your name?" asked Sammy.

"What is *your* name?" replied the girl.

"Sammy. My name is Sammy."

"I like that name. That will be my name."

"No, you can't use my name you have to use your name."

"Why? Is Sammy a bad word?"

"No, not at all. But your name is special. You know the word special?"

"My name is Special? I don't like that name *Special*. I want the Sammy name."

"What name did your mother call you?"

"No name."

'No name? Why not?"

"Because when I baby I don't know yet. When I get bigger and I know then I find my own name, like Sammy. I like Sammy. Is Sammy a bad name?"

"No, that's not a bad name. Your daddy taught you to speak English?"

"Yes. And he name me Bertha. I no like that name. Too many that name on island."

"Why did he teach you to speak English?" asked Sammy.

"So I could talk to him. He say he was *'merican sailor*. He dead now. We ate him."

"What! You ate your father? Are you serious?" exclaimed Sammy.

"What word *serious*? I no like that name *serious*."

"Why would you eat your father? Why would you eat anybody?" asked Sammy.

"It good thing for to honor him. We eat him in feast with funglu and happy good time."

"Um... all of him?"

"Yes, all mostly. Not much to eat when all people come so we have pig and fish too. Some parts of daddy not so good so we throw them in the ocean."

"My god is this possible, am I still in the 21st century?" mumbled an amazed Sammy.

"*God? Goddamn*," said the girl. "I know that word. Is goddamn good word?"

"How about we just call you Sammy Two?"

"*Sammytu*. That a good fuckin' word name. I like Sammytu."

Chapter 11

Oval Office White House

"I don't get it. How the hell did everybody find out about that damn island?" asked the President. "I thought it was confidential, top secret. I thought it was *Top Secret*."

Everyone at the meeting sat silent while they tried to form an answer that would leave the impression they were doing their job and they weren't responsible. In attendance in the Oval Office was a large collection of important CYA individuals that included the Secretary of State, the Chairman of the Joint Chiefs of Staff of the Military, the Director of the Central Intelligence Agency, the National Security Advisor, the Attorney General of the United States, the Secretary of Defense, Secretary of Energy, the Director of National Intelligence, the Secretary of Homeland Security, the Ambassador to the United Nations, the Director of the Federal Bureau of Investigation, and the Vice President.

"Well. Anybody got anything to say?" asked the President.

The President wasn't your average President in the average sense of the word. He was pretty much just a regular guy who got fed up with all the idiots in Washington so he decided to run for president. Fortunately for him, damn near the entire voting public felt the same way and he got elected.

"Well?" he said.

"Yes, I think the Steelers are going to win the Super Bowl," said the Chairman of the Joint Chiefs.

"No way. Going to be the Patriots all the way," said the National Security Advisor. "I'll put money on it."

"I'll take a piece of that," said the President. "Put me in for a few hundred. But first I want to know how the hell the info on that damn island got leaked. Anybody have anything to say?"

"Yes. It's too crowded in here Mr. President. Why don't we move this meet to the conference room," suggested the Vice President.

"We have a conference room?" said the President.

"Of course, so why don't we move this meeting there?"

"Because then we have to invite the media and I don't want those bastards knowing about any of this."

"But they already know about this," replied the VP

"It also means I'd have to feed you folks lunch and I already ate lunch. Besides, you can buy your own damn lunch. This is the White House, not a homeless shelter or a charity house. You all get paid good money so buy your own damn lunch."

"Half the countries in the world might disagree about this not being a charity house, Mr. President," said the Secretary of State, humorously.

"Only half?" laughed the President. "Have to fix that don't we? Too damn many countries on this planet with their hands out. Bullshit."

"Can't disagree with that," said the Chairman of the Joint Chiefs. "About the Patriots, I mean."

"Uh huh. Now, back to business. Who the hell leaked about the island?" said the President.

"I think it leaked from NASA," said the Vice President.

"No. It came from a spy in the Internal Revenue Service," said the Director of the FBI. "He tried to get away when we discovered him so we shot him."

"You shot him?" asked the President. "Why the hell did you shoot him? You have any idea what a damn media stink that will cause? And if he's black it will turn into a racist issue. Every time I turn around I'm being accused of being a racist. God almighty I hate to see what's going to happen when the NAACP finds out we've been dealing with extra terrestrials for half a century. They'll be raising hell because the little space people aren't black enough. Don't they know that gray lives matter to?"

"Not a problem," said the Secretary of Homeland Security. We stuck him in solitary confinement down in

GITMO after we shot him. Under torture he admitted he knew about the island but all he would say was they have great Margaritas and a wonderful masseuse named Peaches who does the special for an extra twenty bucks. Oh, and he said please don't tell his wife. He also admitted to messing around with all the Tea Party exemption applications so they would be delayed or denied. Real nasty piece of work that one."

"He said that?" asked the President.

"Yes sir."

"Are we talking about the same island?" asked the President.

"We'll soon know. I've sent some agents to the island in question to verify," said the Secretary of Homeland Security.

"When?"

"Three days ago."

"Where did they go?"

"You know, the island. The one west of Barbados."

"Have they reported anything yet?" asked the President.

"They have. They reported that our spy told the truth. That the margaritas are supreme and so is Peaches," said the Secretary of Homeland Security. "I'm thinking of going there myself to double check their results."

The President shook his head. "You know I've never understood why President Bush established an entirely new agency after 9/11... or why the hell he called it Homeland Security. I'm beginning to think the only thing you people secure is your jobs, your travel vouchers, and your budget, and all the while you think a recently created monolithic bureaucracy is going to stop world terror. Shit man, I thought that's what our military is supposed to do."

"Me too," agreed the Secretary of Defense. "All those bureaucrats do is fuck with peoples' rights. Easier to just shoot them and get it over with."

"If we shot everybody then we wouldn't know anything," replied the Secretary of Homeland Security. "That's why we have a huge budget, so we can lean stuff."

"And then shoot them," said the Secretary of Defense.

"You got the wrong man," said the National Security Advisor.

"Oh yeah? Well then who the hell was it?" asked the Secretary of Homeland Security.

"It was that blind guy who works the snack bar in the Capitol Building basement. We suspected him so we bugged his house, his car, the snack bar, his girlfriend, and his dog because we had info that he knew everything about the island. But he says the only island he has ever seen was his home island of Haiti when he was three years old. We're pretty sure that's a smoke screen or cover-up. These guys are pretty crafty and can't always be believed."

"I didn't know you bugged him. Why didn't I know? I'm the Attorney Genera. I don't think that was legal," said the Attorney General. "Why didn't I know?"

"This is a national crisis," replied the National Security Advisor. "Who cares about legalities during a national crisis?"

"This is a national crisis?" asked the Secretary of Defense. "Why didn't anybody tell me? If they had told me I wouldn't have made reservations for a golf weekend at Pebble Beach. I don't show up and I lose my two thousand dollar deposit."

"Now that's a crisis," said the Chairman of the Joint Chiefs.

"It's always a national crisis. That's why we're here because there's always a national crisis," said the Director of the CIA."

"What are you, some kind of Democrat who thrives on imaginary national crisis?" asked the VP.

"Uh, I was a Democrat until I got this job. Now I'm a... conservative Baptist," replied the Director of the CIA.

"It's not a problem," said the Secretary of Homeland Security. "We stuck the snack bar guy in GITMO in solitary confinement. Shouldn't be any more leaks."

"Who needs more leaks? The info about the island is all over God's creation now. All they need is the New York Times," piped in the Secretary of Energy. "The important thing is who the hell is going to get to that uranium first."

"Did you torture him?" the President asked of the National Security Advisor.

"Torture who?" asked the Secretary of Homeland Security.

"The guy at GITMO," said the President.

"Which one?" asked the Director of the CIA.

"The blind snack bar guy in the basement," replied the President.

"Of course not."

"Why not?" asked the President.

"Nobody in our agency has the heart to torture a blind guy, especially one with leg braces from childhood polio," replied the Secretary of Homeland Security. "Besides, he's a member of the Service Employees International Union and the American Federation of Government Employees, and the Urban League, and the PTA, and he's black."

"Yeah, I see your point. So why not send for that National Guard girl that tortured all those Hodgies in Abu Ghraib. I bet she would do it."

"I don't think that's a good idea and I don't think it's legal," said the Attorney General. "Besides, I think she's still in prison… maybe."

"Yeah, we can put her in the Park Service and pretend she caught this guy in the bushes trying to screw a Boy Scout or something and claim she tortured him to find out if there are any other victims. The public never defends or sympathizes with those kind of people."

"But I really don't think that's legal," said the Attorney General.

"Shit man, you don't think anything is legal," said the Secretary of Defense. Everyone around the room nodded their heads in agreement and the Attorney General cowered silently back into his chair. He wasn't a man who liked conflict and in fact never wanted to be Attorney General in the first place except for the fact his wife threatened to leave him if he declined. She wanted to maintain her status at the country club and his position in the government allowed her to do exactly that.

"Well god damnit, who the hell leaked the shit?" asked an angry President.

They all sat silent again until a fresh voice came from across the room. "You did, Mr. President."

Everyone turned and looked and remained silent because they knew by experience that this particular person, the only woman in the room, was almost always correct. It was Stella May Fulgenzi, the Ambassador to the United Nations. She was always the most informed cabinet member of the group, even though they weren't even sure she was a cabinet member, and could always say whatever she wanted in the company of the President because she was a five foot eight blonde hotty who melted the President's brain with her very presence. In fact, she melted the brain and the heart of everybody in the room.

"You leaked it, Mr. President, when you briefed those Congressional leaders with those idiot Democrats and that dumb ass Republican Senator Yorkie. Bad call, sir," said Ambassador Fulgenzi.

The President blushed, sat back in his chair, then said, "Oh."

Again, no one said a word until Ambassador Fulgenzi finished.

"So here's the situation Mr. President; according to the info floating around the UN, the Russians, the Chinese, the Israelis, possibly the North Koreans, possibly Iran, a Texas oil tycoon, and somehow that crazy woman, um… Sammy Sinclair, are all hell bent on claiming your little island," stated the Ambassador. "Oh, and there's a rumor that the Boy Scouts of America would like to claim it for the use of their annual Jamboree location, although another rumor says that the executives of the organization want to use it in the off season for a for-profit gay vacation destination playground… after they build an airport with a government grant."

"Hmmmm," said the President. "This is starting to sound serious, yep, pretty damn serious. Gentlemen, um and lady, how soon can we put a team on that island?"

"A team of what?" asked the VP.

"A team. A military team," clarified the President. "What other kind of team is there."

"Well, there's analyst teams and accounting teams and campaign teams and the First Lady's wardrobe team, and the White House social planning team and…"

"Not that shit. I mean a kick-ass military team," interrupted the President.

"I can have troops in the air in six hours Mr. President," offered the Secretary of Defense. "We anticipated this and have already prepped an expeditionary force for this purpose."

"No no. Too damn big and obvious," said the President.

"How about a SEAL team, fast and furious. We can call it Operation…"

"You don't have to call it anything, god damn It! Every time you people start calling shit silly ass names it turns into a massive operation and a ten year war. I don't want any damn war. If I wanted a war I'd ask for a war. Did I ask for a war? No. I just want our flag on that tiny damn island. That's all. Just stick a fucking flag in the ground and declare it a protectorate, that's all. Is that too much to ask? Is it? Do we even know where this thing is located?"

"Yes," said the Secretary of State. "We got the exact GPS Coordinates from the New York Times and confirmed it with CNN.

"But that's a mighty high value tiny island," said Ambassador Fulgenzi. "Should be secured ASAP, Mr. President."

"Yes, Stella, I mean Ambassador, I suppose you're right," agreed the President.

"Of course I'm right, sir," replied Ambassador Fulgenzi as she glared at the group of men standing about the office.

"Let's send a team of something out there to plant an American flag and do it pretty damn quick," said the President. "I want to get this crisis out of the way before it becomes a crisis. And Stella, I mean Ambassador Fulgenzi, I want your legs… I mean, you to coordinate all this and go with them to keep the peace. Oh, and you go too Attorney General Morgan. Need you to keep everything legal."

"But Mr. President, I don't think any of this is legal," said a nervous Attorney General.

"Well hell, Morgan, that's why you've got to be there, because if it isn't legal it's up to you to make it legal. That's what you lawyers do isn't it?" stated the President.

Attorney General Morgan thought a moment, trying very hard to remember if he had learned that very concept somewhere, anywhere, during his education at Harvard Law School. He even searched his memories of the pizza joint where he went with his law school friends to discuss law and getting laid, but he pulled a blank.

"Don't worry Morgan. I got your back," said Ambassador Fulgenzi, who by the way was also an experienced lawyer. In fact everyone in the President's cabinet was either a lawyer or former high level military officer because in the Federal government, to be anything other than a lawyer or general or admiral was considered to be an idiot. Only members of Congress and a few well connected politically appointed heads of bureaucracies were tolerated and excused for being legally stupid… as long as they didn't do anything.

The group disbanded and, while departing the Oval Office out in the hall of the West Wing, UN Ambassador Stella Fulgenzy immediately took charge and started barking orders. "Admiral, I want a full complement of Delta boys geared up and ready to lift off first thing in the morning," she said to the Secretary of Defense. "We will transfer to choppers in Hawaii and fly to a carrier as near to that island as possible without being detected or causing any concern to other countries. From there we will HALO onto the island. All other plans will be formulated on board the ship. Is that understood?"

"I was hoping we wouldn't decide this until after lunch," said the Admiral.

"Lunch?" said Ambassador Fulgenzi.

"Yes, lunch. Would you care to join us? We are going to…"

"Fuck your lunch, Admiral. I want a team of Deltas packin' and rackin' ASAP. Got that? Wheels up by dawn."

"I'd prefer to assign SEALs Miss Ambassador. They're the best in the Navy and…"

"I said Delta, Admiral. Ever since that Obama idiot ran his mouth about SEAL Team 6 after they snuffed Osama bin Laden those guys have been under a spotlight. Hell they even got their own movies and a regular TV show. I don't want primadonnas and media heroes, Admiral, I want proven kick ass soldiers. I want *Army Delta*."

"What about Chuck Norris?" asked the Chairman of the Joint Chiefs. "He made two movies with Lee Majors about the Delta Force."

"Yeah but nobody remembers those flicks," said the Secretary of Homeland Security.

"Did you say HALO jump? Like from an airplane jump?" asked Attorney General Morgan.

"That's right, wheels up at dawn. Now get on it," barked Ambassador Fulgenzi.

"Ummm… yes ma'am," replied the Secretary of Defense.

"Uh, I think I have a dentist appointment," said a nervous Attorney General Morgan.

"You think? Fine, go to your phony damn dentist appointment you little pussy. Don't need your ass anyway," said the Ambassador as she walked off.

"But the President said…"

"Yeah yeah, no sweat. I got that," said the Ambassador, waiving him off as she walked away.

After Ambassador Stella Fulgenzi was out of ear range, "I'll be damned," said the Admiral, "I bet she calls cadence when she's having sex."

"Wouldn't bother me," said the Director of the FBI.

"I think you'd have to ask the President about that," said the National Security Advisor.

"What… what the… Did you bug the Ambassador? Did you bug the President?" asked a nervous Attorney General Morgan.

The National Security Advisor smiled slyly. "Damn Morgan, you sure are paranoid." He then turned and winked to the Director of the FBI who in fact did the bugging for the National Security Advisor. After Attorney General Morgan walked away he said to the FBI

Director, "Good thing that little twerp doesn't know that we bug everybody in the government."

"Yeah," laughed the Director. "Then he would know his wife is screwing the tennis pro at the club."

Chapter 12

It's Not Your Island!

It was late night, somewhere around 0130 hours, with no moon making it extremely dark and advantageous for the team of Black Ass deserters from Madagascar. The muffled engine of the zodiac sprayed water into the air as it flopped through the surf to eventually reach the calm waters of a large lagoon. When they approached the island they slowed the boat to a near silent cruise and the ten passengers perked up, becoming alert to any danger. The tropical growth and palms that hung out over the lagoon were at first ghostly, but later began to embrace and even welcome the invaders as it hid them from the shore.

"What's that?" whispered one of the FBI agents.

"What's what?" asked Crazy Bob.

"What's what what?" came another voice from the darkness in the rear of the boat.

"That smell," said the FBI agent. "What the hell is that smell?"

Corky pulled his lantern from his combat vest, set it to low beam and turned it on. When he aimed it towards the center of the boat he discovered Herpie pigging out on a slice of pizza.

"Herpie, what the hell are you doing?" he whispered.

"I'm eating pizza. What the hell you think I'm doing," replied Herpie.

"You're going to give us away, you idiot," complained the FBI agent.

"Hey, you heard the man. He said nobody lives on this island except a bunch of pigs. And I'm hungry," said Herpie.

"Yeah, well you're going to have every damn pig on this island coming down on us when they catch a whiff of that damn pizza," said the FBI guy.

"Where the hell did you get pizza?" asked Crazy Bob.

"On the Texan's yacht, where do you think? The chefs cooked it up for me. Those guys can cook anything, man. You know how long it's been since I had a pizza?" said Herpie. "First bite wasn't that great though. Got some of that face camo shit on it. It was dark and I missed my mouth. Man, you can't imagine how good this shit is once you get past the camo. I mean it's got anchovies and pepperoni and cheese and olives and mushrooms and everything. Those guys on that yacht can really cook, especially that Italian guy."

"Enjoy it while you can dumb ass because you're going to be living on pig meat, fish, and coconuts pretty soon," said Crazy Bob.

"How about pineapples, mate? You think there's some pineapples?" asked MacDougal. "I can rig up some pretty damn good grub with pineapple. And bananas too."

"Hey, shut the hell up," whispered the FBI guy. "You're going to blow the mission."

"Yeah," laughed Herpie with a mouth full of pizza. "Don't want to run the risk of getting shot by a wild pig or a sniper koocan bird."

"That's *toucan* dummy. *Toucan*," said one of the deserters.

"Hey, look. Up there at the end of the lagoon," said T-Bone.

They cut the engine and the gang grew silent and watched as the boat drifted slowly toward what appeared to be some dim flickering lights. Jimmy "T-Bone" Carter was the South Georgia country boy who was posted on the nose of the zodiac. He readied his weapon and strained to look through the darkness to make sense of what was ahead. Lights, he thought, it was lights. "Torches. Tiki torches."

"Torches? Looks like we have some pretty advanced pigs on this island," whispered Corky.

They all readied their weapons, locked and loaded and firmed up their courage to jump into the first bit of combat they had seen since Vietnam. Two men in the rear pulled out the paddles and used them to stop the progress of the zodiac. After they did, the entire group slid off the sides of the boat into the water and began to slowly swim to shore in the direction of the lights. As they swam they spread out and silently climbed ashore where they could now see a small village. Once on dry ground they all looked to Corky who gave orders by hand signal, telling them to surround the place and hold until he told them on their com sets to move in.

Once in position they began to slowly close in but were temporarily halted when they heard the soft and pleasant sound of people singing. Corky told them to halt and stay put while he crawled through the brush to get a closer look. When he reached a point where he could see people he froze, then stood and stared. When the others saw him they decided to do the same, assuming all was well. They joined him as he walked into the village.

Sammytu was the first to see them. "Holy shit!" she cried out and stood surprised. The rest of the islanders rose to their feet and faced the intruders. They looked both bewildered and curious. And of course the very first thing that the deserter boys noticed was the island people were all *buck-ass naked*. From within the group came a nude midget (with a fanny pack) who immediately raised his arms in surrender. Finally from inside one of the native hooches came a very naked and appealing Slammin' Sammy Sinclair and... the stare off began.

"Sorry, gentlemen," Sammy said finally in a stern direct order. "You must turn around and head back where you came from. This is not your island."

"I beg to differ, ma'am," replied Corky. "This island is not internationally recorded as belonging to any country or listed as any sovereignty, in fact it doesn't exist. Until tonight that is. Now it belongs to us."

"Sorry, gentlemen, but as you can see this island is occupied and is called Wassi… um… Wassimaso.. ah shit. It's called Whatchamacalit Island and is the sovereign nation of the Whatchamacalit people."

"Whatchamacalit? Hah, are you serious lady? We are declaring this our island on behalf of uh, the uh… Black Ass… Corporation."

"*Serious*. Sammy there that word again. What mean *serious*?" said Sammytu.

"Oh yeah, and just what's the name of this island that you think is your island? Huh? Tell me that," challenged Sammy.

"We declare this is now the island of… um, Black Ass," said Crazy Bob.

"Is that a bad word name?" asked Sammytu.

Just as Sammy was about to dispute Corky's declaration and begin kicking his ass she paused when all the natives started walking to the invading force. The deserters were paralyzed with amazement because they had never come up against an enemy of lovely buck ass naked people… and a midget… and a hot naked American chick.

"Hey man, that chick looks kind of like Raquel Welch," observed Herpie.

"That's not her," replied Corky.

"I didn't say that was her. I said she looks like her."

"Yeah, you're right. But that's not her."

"But I didn't say it was her, I said…" he paused when the people surrounded them and began to touch and remove the combat gear attached to their combat vest and drop it on the ground. Before they knew it the Black Ass gang had been relieved of all their gear and weapons and in fact were beginning to be undressed by the natives.

"Hey man. What the hell they doing?" said one of the FBI agents.

"Who cares, mate," said MacDougal. "I'm thinking this is a good thing. No harm, no foul says I."

"What's the problem dude?" said T-Bone to the FBI agent. "Hell, man, at our age you got to get it when you can, you know? But then y'all FBI boys wouldn't know that yet, so just kick back and cool it will ya? Trust me son, the clock don't stop for nobody."

What the Black Ass gang didn't know was that all 67 islanders had just partaken in a luau and eaten one of their favorite relatives, complete with lots of funglu sauce, and all that funglu smothered family sushi was starting to kick in. Now they were undressing the Black Ass boys and offering them funglu laced coconut milk. Needless to say everyone, deserters and islanders, ended up in piles of writhing bodies until dawn.

"Hot damn, this stuff is better than Three Horses Beer," said one of the FBI guys.

Hidden in the nearby undergrowth camouflaged and wrapped in a mess of leafy branches laid two observers, one whispering to the other saying, "What he mean Three Horses?"

The man next to him shook his head, confused, and replied, "I think he mean screwing these pretty women much better than screwing three horses."

"I think I agree," came a whispered reply from a voice four feet away in the dark.

"Me too," came another voice from the darkness.

"Yes," came another.

"You bet, me too," said the voice furthest away in the underbrush.

"How would you know unless you screwed horses?" came one of the voices in the darkness.

Suddenly all the voices went silent and there were no more comments for a long moment until, "I bet Chun-mei Fu Quang screws horses."

And all the faceless voices in the dark giggled.

Chapter 13

Meanwhile Back at the Ranch

In front of the great big fireplace in the great big great room in his great big house on his great big ranch stood the great big Tex the Big Bopper. On the great big leather sofa in the center of the room sat his millennial tech head Alvin wearing headphones and punching on the keyboard of a laptop computer.

"Well, ya got anythin' yet?" grumbled Tex.

The tech head didn't respond.

"I said you got anythin'?" repeated Tex.

Alvin still didn't respond and finally Tex walked over and slapped him on the head. The millennial marvel startled, looked up, and removed the headphones.

"I said, YOU GOT ANYTHIN' YET?" yelled Tex.

"No sir. Nothing I can understand," replied Alvin.

"What the hell's that mean?"

"Well, sir, they're sending for sure but all I can hear is a bunch of moaning and groaning and such."

"Are you tellin' me my boys on that island are moanin' and groanin' in pain and dying? Is that what you're tellin' me?"

"Yes sir. I mean no sir. I mean I don't really know, sir."

"Son, talkin' to you is like tryin' to put together a jigsaw puzzle made up of three different pichers. The parts jus' don't fit. Now let's start all over." Tex took a breather then said, "Now I want you to tell me exactly what yer hearin' from my boys on that there island on that thar radio thing on your head."

Tech head Alvin decided not to answer and instead put the signal on speaker. Out flowed a myriad of sounds, none of which he could identify primarily because he was a tech-head and a 27 year old virgin. But Tex on the other hand has been around the block quite a few times and readily recognized the sounds he was hearing, although he'd never heard them from so many people at one time. "God damn," exclaimed Tex. "No wonder those boys all deserted the war. Ain't no place in the US Army for those kinna men."

The millennial tech head looked at Tex confused because he had no idea what he was talking about.

"Okay now son, you tried talking to those boys?" asked Tex.

"Yes sir. A couple times actually."

"Well, what the hell'd they say?"

"Um... I couldn't understand anything they said sir. It sounded like gibberish mixed with Russian, Chinese,

English, French, Indian, and a whole bunch of other languages. I've never heard anything like it, not that I'm a linguist or anything. But the odd thing is they always sounded like children. I don't know what to tell you, sir, except maybe they're being tortured or something."

"Tortured? Tortured? Well God damn son we sure as hell can't have any a that. Not with my boys. Pack your shit, son. We're headin' west to rescue our boys."

In the village on Whatchamacalit Island the sounds of moans and groans of rapture poured out through the walls of the grass huts and permeated the air. Amidst all the huts sat the little children of the village playing with the combat gear belonging to the Black Ass boys and in the center of them all sat a small girl who was thoroughly enjoying playing with the radio. Each time she flipped a certain switch a small red light would come on and she would laugh uncontrollably. Often the other children would join in and they would all begin jibber-jabbering and laughing and the sound of their joy would mix with the sounds of sexual ecstasy drifting from the huts and it would all find its way into the microphone of the combat radio from which a signal was being linked up to a satellite and then down to the great big ranch in Texas.

"Yes sirrreeee," said Tex as he stepped up into his helicopter. "We gotta save our boys and make sure it's my island. Myyyy island, I say! I'm gonna call it… *Yellow Rose Island* after my great grandma. Now that there was one hell of a sweet ol' lady."

Chapter 14

Putin's Puppet

During the same moonless dark night, just off the northern shore of Whatchamacalit Island there surfaced from the depths of the ocean a very large elongated black oval shaped craft. After it settled on the surface, a hatch at the top of the bridge sporting a small white, blue, and red emblem of the Russian flag opened and out came three men.

On the lower deck a larger hatch opened and some crewmen were quickly pulling out a raft. Following the raft, up through the hatch there came another man who, when the raft was ready and in the water, turned and looked up to the bridge and saluted. All three men on the bridge quickly returned his salute.

"He has great courage," said the boat's Captain.

"He is facing a very difficult ordeal," said his first officer.

"Vould you accept such a difficult task, Captain?" asked the Chief of the Boat.

"It is our duty to serve without question, but... no, not on your life. Putin is an ass and I would not participate in one of his money grabbing follies... unless he cut me in," replied the captain. "I just took this mission so we can stop off in Singapore and have a little fun for a few days.

Following the old formality of a salute, their passenger then climbed down into the raft with five other men, one on the motor and the other four, armed with Kalashnikov rifles, were positioned at the side of the raft. The small boat sped swiftly to shore where their passenger quickly jumped out onto the beach, looked about and then turned back to his comrades who to his surprise where already thirty yards away and heading quick smart back to their submarine.

"Эй! Что происходит? Куда, черт возьми, вы идете?" he called, meaning, *"Hey! Vas es goink on? Vare the hell are you goink?"* He quickly grabbed his radio and called up the Captain of the submarine. "Capitan," he pleaded. "Vas are you doink. Chu can not leaf me here alone. How vill I survife? Vas am I to do?"

"You will do your duty as do ve all," replied the Captain.

"But, but, but..."

"You should really do something about that stutter, comrade. It is not becoming of a true Russian operative," said the Captain. "Farewell and good luck."

Disappointed, the Russian stood alone on the beach and watched as his lifeline and protection submerged beneath the ocean waves. "Ты, сын суки, мать, чертовски задница, косаки-ублюдки!" he yelled, meaning, "&^%#$*&@#"

There he stood alone on what he thought was supposed to be a deserted island. Alone with his cracked eyeglasses, alone with one bottle of vodka, alone with two tins of caviar and cheddar cheese peanut butter crackers he picked up in America, and alone with a partially melted chocolate Snickers bar, a radio made in China that didn't work very well, one change of underwear, a Swiss Army Knife, and a fold up sign to be posted on a tree that states in Russian, Эта земля является собственностью Владимира Владимировича Путина. Meaning,

THIS LAND IS THE PROPERTY OF VLADIMIR VLADIMIROVICH PUTIN. TRESPASSERS WILL BE SHOT!

There Borris Bolufski stood all alone on a mission to lay claim to Whatchamacalit Island for Vladimir Putin. Borris Bolufski, Russia's pride and joy and very own version of the klutzy Pink Panther.

Chapter 15

I Muffed It at the UN!

The Israeli Ambassador to the United Nations was at an all time high because on this day he was going to speak to the general assembly and what he had to say had absolutely nothing to do with those damn Muslims as usual. It was indeed his day to shine. He had no complaints about Muslim terrorists, no complaints about the UN meddling in Israel's business about killing Muslim radicals, no complaints about the UN spending too much money on the UN instead of Israel, and no complaints about UN peacekeeping troops who just sit around in their silly colored helmets and don't do any peacekeeping. Instead he was going to announce the addition of a newly discovered body of land that Israel is welcoming into its family. Today, as per his instructions from Prime Minister Malachi Manheim (who received his inspiration from his wife Samara so she could visit her sister in Miami), he was going to announce that through diligent work and years of exploration Israel has discovered an uncharted island, and according to maritime law, they are going to claim it. As for what maritime law, they weren't really sure. Just the same, with great pomp and *circumcision*, and self serving pride, the Israelites were going to claim Whatchamacalit Island, the island that will henceforth be known as the *Isle of Golda*, in honor of their distinguished former national leader, Golda Meir.

Of course this name was just a play on words being gold was the primary object of the moment. But alternatively it was this moment that was going to get them the goodies in the form of a billion bucks and a half dozen F-35 Lightning Joint Strike Fighters. That is if the United States reacted as they usually do. On the other hand, should the US fail to perform as usual then Prime Minister Manheim would be much like the US President Thomas Jefferson who increased the size of his country with a single purchase. Manheim would increase the size of his country by 25 square miles of gold and diamonds and even oil (if they can keep it on the QT), and unlike the west bank, it should be trouble free.

As the Israeli Ambassador was making his announcement a voice came from the assembly. "NO!" cried the voice from the massive group of international representatives. "You lie. This is not your island. It is Russia's island. We have already posted claim and our representative stands on that ground as we speak," echoed the man's voice throughout the grand room.

"I assure you Ambassador Gorkov, the island has been legally claimed by the sovereign state of Israel and as such you could not have claimed or settled it.

"This cannot be true," came another voice of dissent. "This cannot be true because this island you speak of belongs to the people of China," called out the Chinese Ambassador who actually worked for Chun-mei Fu Quang and would probably be assassinated if he failed this debate.

"Once again China claims what is not theirs. Not to mention the theft of all the industrial secrets of the free world," said the Japanese Ambassador.

"And from whom do you steal your trade secrets? Shall we say *everyone*. The sun would not rise over Japan were it not for your devious traits," replied the Chinese Ambassador.

"Gentlemen please," said the Swiss Ambassador. "I feel we should somehow bring this unscheduled debate to a conclusion. Perhaps we Swiss could claim the island and declare it a neutral place. Why, we could even use it as a banking center for the, well… everyone."

"I think I can help there," said the current US Ambassador Dr. Jerry Julobondi. He was Ambassador Stella Fulgenzi's alternate and was well prepared for such a public conflict.

"Please do," pleaded the sophisticated and articulate Secretary General of the UN Mr. Ombalega Motoo Wambaga of the tiny country of Suyapa in Africa. "All in this assembly would be most grateful if you would do exactly that."

No one was sure how or why Wambaga was ever elected to the position of Secretary General because Suyapa was a tiny little country that most people in the world have never heard of. But Suyapa, though very, very small with no resources and a lazy population of only 160,000 people, was actually a very rich country. Many at the UN thought this was because Wambaga was the Secretary General of the UN and continuously declared a national crisis or disease that threatened his people and the world, which in turn generated lots and lots of money from the UN, and the US, and movie stars and rock and roll singers. That was the obvious payoff. Many others thought it was because of the strange witch doctor that accompanied him every minute of the day and night. Whenever anyone challenged or disagreed with Wambaga his witch doctor would put the hairy eyeball on them and they would simply grow silent and walk away. When the witch doctor put the double whammy on them they would then agree with anything and everything Wambaga desired. Hence he kept getting reelected to the controlling position of Secretary General of the United Nations. He was also recognized by his peers because of how his country maintained an even numbered population which resulted in no overcrowding or hunger. What most of them didn't know however was how the people of Suyapa would go machete apeshit once a decade and one half of the people would chop up the other half. Hence the controlled population.

The American Ambassador stood and approached the Israeli speaker who stood behind the podium above. "Tell me, Mr. Ambassador," asked the American. "You declare this island to be the property, or at least a protectorate of Israel?"

"Yes, of course," replied the Israeli.

"So tell us, what was the name of the island before you changed it to Golda?"

"Uh… it was called Wassi… um… Wassimaso... or something."

"You really don't know?"

"I just can't pronounce it. So what?"

"Then please, Mr. Ambassador, would you be so kind as to tell all of us how you found this island and where it lies out there in the Pacific Ocean?"

"Um… I can't. I don't know."

"Have you seen this island?"

"No."

"Has anybody from Israel ever seen this island?"

"I don't know."

"You don't know? Why not? If you are going to announce ownership you should at least be able to offer some photos and a location and maybe even a native or two from this island. And better yet, an explanation why a small country like yours would even want to take the trouble to take on the responsibility of a tiny place on the other side of the world."

The Israeli just shook his head and offered no answers.

"Let me help you, sir. You see what really happened is the United States of America discovered this island via a NASA satellite and we also discovered that it has a number of very valuable resources. The island belongs to no one except a population of pigs and as we speak an expedition of Americans is currently on their way to claim and settle the place in question. That is the way of the world and the history of man. Do you agree, Mr. Ambassador?"

"But you can't do that. I have just announced the ownership of the island for Israel."

"Perhaps you would also like to claim the planet of Mars for Israel since you seem to feel it is not necessary for you to actually go there. You might even wish to through in Venus and Jupiter for good measure."

"Don't be ridiculous," countered the Israeli Ambassador.

"It is no more ridiculous than what you are trying to do here today, is it not?"

The Israeli squirmed uncomfortably.

"Sorry, Ambassador. But in my country there is an old saying. It goes, *'finders keepers losers weepers'* and the finders is the United States. And there is an old edict that says, and I quote, *'possession is nine-tenths of the law'* or something like that.

"No. No, no, no," spoke up the French Ambassador. "The island belongs to France and has belonged to France since 1804."

"Oh, so we have a new player in the game. Can you prove that Mr. French Ambassador," asked the American.

The Frenchman hesitated because he had no proof and knew there was none to be found anywhere in France because they had destroyed it all, and the only proof that existed walked out the door of the French archives with Slammin' Sammy Sinclair and Chow Chow, not because they were thieves but because the French copy machine was on the fritz and had been on the fritz for almost four years. "No sir," replied the Frenchman sadly. "I'm afraid all the records were destroyed in the war. So I beg this assembly to find in our favor out of recognizing and understanding the truth when you hear it and sympathy for the French people who were invaded and suffered the consequences of war by the Germans who ravaged our history and our records."

"What!" came another voice from the assembly. "You dare to blame us Germans for your obvious inadequacy? We did not ravage your country and your records. You just rolled over and surrendered before the fight even began. All we took from you were your Jews and your women."

"You would have this great body here to believe you German's did no harm to Mother France! How dare you. The entire world knows what you have done, you NAZI bastards."

The French Ambassador was a master chef by profession but it was revealed during a presentation and bid to host the Olympics that he was also quite an orator when he was arguing that the Russians and British made lousy food and the French created the finest in the world and for that reason alone the French should win the bid to host the Olympics. Actually, like most French chefs his cooking was fairly mediocre but with his very cool accent he was very good at convincing people that his cuisine was beyond excellent. What he didn't know was that both a Russian and Englishman were on the Olympic Committee and took the food insult personally. It was later proven that he may have been correct because the Russians (after Putin bribed the Olympic committee) won the bid to host the games at which a thousand international athletes became sicker than a dog from bad Russian food and water, including the Russian McDonalds and later when the games were in London most of the Olympic athletes quickly tired of fish and chips and began searching out international restaurants like Pizza Hut and Subway. With his country finally realizing the chef was correct about French and Russian food, he was made a national hero and subsequently became the French Ambassador to the United Nations in New York - where he almost always eats at the Manhattan Chick-fil-A.

The Frenchman's delivery and words were smooth and moving in spite of the German's opposition. He knew all he had to do was call the German a NAZI and he would win the argument because to this day nobody likes the NAZIs. And the American could see he was fast winning over the UN assembly, reminding him of when the UN was swayed to ignore the wholesale slaughter that took place in Cambodia that took millions of lives. And so he wondered what his President would do and then went for it. "I'm sorry, Frenchie, but you got no grounds to stand on. Neither do you, you lying Jew, or the lying Chinese or the lying Russians or anybody else. The simple fact is we got it and if you want it you're going to have to fight us for it. See you on the battlefield folks."

With those final words the American Ambassador turned and walked out mumbling under his breath, "UN my ass. This damn organization is nothing but a dark hole full of bullshit rhetoric where money disappears. It's a waste of damn time is what it is, as useful as tits on a bull hog. What am I doing here? It's a waste of *my* time. I could have been the CEO of Enron or Yahoo with one hell of a golden parachute. Shit. After this crap I'll be lucky to end up teaching Political Science at a community college in Jersey."

Chapter 16

Banzai!

The Prime Minister of Japan entered the room and waiting around the table were his cabinet of Ministers of State. They all bowed and took their seats.

"Honorable Daichi, you have called this meeting. What have you to say?" asked the Prime Minister.

Daichi stood, bowed, and spoke. "It is in regards to the island disputed upon in the United Nations. This island is abundantly blessed with gold, diamonds, oil, and uranium. I am proposing that we take it."

"Take it from who?" asked the Prime Minister.

"From no one," Honorable Prime Minister. "But possibly from the Americans."

"How? Is this island for sale?"

"No, Admirable Prime Minister, but it is so enormously wealthy it would be worth any effort to obtain it."

"Effort such as?" questioned the Prime Minister.

"A military Banzai," replied Daichi. "Our troops have been preparing for many, many years for such a mission."

"What troops?" asked the Prime Minister.

"Our many soldiers in the Royal Army of the Japanese People."

"We do not have a Royal Army of the Japanese People, Minister Daichi," stated the Prime Minister.

"But Prime Minister, what about all those…"

"We do not have a Royal Army of the Japanese People, Minister Daichi. That was part of the terms of our surrender to the United States in 1945. Therefore all those troops in the Royal Army of the Japanese People that we have we do not have. Understood?"

"But we could…"

"No Army," repeated the Prime Minister.

"Why do we not just buy it?" asked one of the other Ministers of State. "Like when we bought half of Hawaii and Hollywood. The Americans don't care. They will sell anything for the right price."

"But we could…"

"We could do *what,* Minister Daichi? Take an island away from the Americans so they can drop another large fucking bomb on our honorable asses? Are you serious? Been there, tried that, end of discussion. Didn't work out very well. The answer is no."

"But…"

"NO."

Chapter 17

Colonel Bitch-Wife

Wake up! I want you to take the kids to school."

Robert E. Lee Fairfield opened one eye and looked toward the window. Noticing there was no light he easily assumed it was still night time. Then it came to him, "What kids," he mumbled after closing his eye. "We don't have any kids."

"They're military kids. *Other peoples'* kids, and it's my turn to drive the little bastards to school. All damn week I get to drive the little shits to school. Do you know why it's my turn to drive the little bastards to school? It's because we – no not we – *you,* are in the Army. And for some goddamn reason you being in the Army means I'm in the army which means that bitch Linda Harper, wife of Colonel Harper, runs all of the Army wives like they're in *your* Army and she's the queen bee who manages our lives because one word from her and she can mess up your career."

"Do we really need to go through all this again... now? Leave me alone, I need to sleep. I had field exercises all night," moaned Robert E. Lee Fairfield. "I don't want to talk about this again. I don't want to drive little bastards to school. I don't want anything except sleep."

"So you just want to play G.I. Joe while all us G.I. wives have to put up with a bunch of shit from some bitch who probably hasn't been laid in a decade. I bet if she got laid she wouldn't be such a bitch. Maybe that Colonel Harper is one of those don't ask don't tell guys."

"How do you know she hasn't been laid?" asked Robert E. as he rolled over and pulled the covers over his head.

"Are you kidding? Have you ever seen that woman? I don't think she could buy a good time for a thousand bucks on the streets of Thailand. If she didn't live on the base she would probably be arrested for public ugly."

"Sometimes you can be very cruel."

"No, I'm very pissed off because I shouldn't have to get up at five, no excuse me, at... 0500... in the morning to drive little shits to school that don't belong to me. I'm not a den mother. Do I look like a damn *den mother* to you? I didn't get a college degree to drive somebody else's little rats to school. I don't like kids. I don't like making cupcakes for kids parties and I don't like attending tea parties where a bunch of frustrated Army wives have to sit around and bite their tongues because they can't tell Colonel Bitch-Wife that she's a bitch while she's telling us what books we should read. Maybe she should be reading the Karma Suture."

"Kama."

"What?"

"Kamasutra. It's Kamasutra, the Indian sex book. *Kamasutra*," he corrected.

"I think you should quit."

"So do I but I can't quit. I haven't completed my enlistment. I can't get out until I've served out my enlistment… and then I run the chance of being recalled."

"Then get kicked out or pretend you're crazy or shoot somebody… like maybe that Colonel Bitch-Wife so you won't have to go back in. Do anything that gets you out of the Army," she yelled as she yanked the covers off the bed. "And get out of bed."

"Hey man, give me the blanket. It's cold!"

"You know why it's cold? I'll tell you why it's cold. It's cold because this is shitty base housing. Not nice base housing like that Colonel Bitch-Wife lives in. Noooo… it's shitty base housing because you're only a Captain. If I could get a job to double our income then we could live off base in a nice house like real people but nooooooooo, that Colonel Bitch-Wife says we can't work because then we would neglect our men who are sacrificing their lives in the service of the finest military in the world. How the hell would she know anything about sacrifice? All she ever sacrifices is my time and… and… her looks."

"Wow. You're really on a roll today. No, wait. It's not day time yet… IS IT?"

"My point exactly. So get your ass out of bed so you can drive those little shits to school. All nine of them."

Robert E. Lee Fairfield was an officer in an Army Delta Force unit based at Fort Meade, Maryland. They were perhaps the least utilized Delta Force unit in all the US Army simply because they were based at Fort Meade, the home of the Presidential retreat of Camp David. Somewhere some time ago some military kiss-ass decided it would be good to have a kick ass military unit readily available in case the President's dog got lost in the woods, which is exactly what happened the only time the unit was ever called to action at Camp David. They found the dog. It was a little rat dog named Consti whose name was short for Constitution, and it was retarded which is why it was lost. The White House never let the public know that Consti was retarded because the political blowback would be unpredictable. Would they say '*Like President like dog*,' or would they say the President was kind and politically correct in caring for a challenged animal? Or would they claim the President made the dog retarded by kicking it every day? Robert E. always thought the dog had only two functions. One was to look cute on TV and get votes and the other was for the President to kick the dog every time he got pissed off when he found out he couldn't do something because of that pain in the ass Constitution – hence the name *Consti*. Just the same, the Delta boys all received a medal for finding the President's retarded dog and one guy even got a Purple Heart because he nearly poked his eye out from a low hanging tree branch. On this occasion however, Robert E. was severely disappointed because he didn't get to kill anybody. It was then he realized he didn't love his wife because on the way home he actually thought about killing her. All she did was bitch and the only thing she could cook was tuna casserole and the casserole was so bad that he could actually justify the murder as self-defense.

Other than that all the unit did was train and then train some more. Sometimes the Army brass would show up with some congressional types and watch them practice. Robert E. thought correctly that their visits were designed to gain more support and a better budget so they could continue to practice. He would always hear the generals argue about how the Navy SEALs got a blank check to purchase and design any gear and weapons they wanted and how they always have the best of everything but Delta had to scrape the bottom of the barrel. Capt. Robert E. never could understand why the Generals would say that because it wasn't true but he did understand that Generals always want more money, probably to keep up the officers' golf courses on the military bases and insure the Officers' Clubs were well stocked with only the finest of booze. He also wondered just how much barrel scraping, if any, went on at the general's level at the Pentagon. To Robert E. it was all bullshit and he didn't actually care as long as the bullets flew straight and his paycheck didn't bounce. Other than that he was simply counting down the days until his discharge and he had reached the point where he welcomed everything the Delta Force threw at him because it usually kept him away from his miserable unhappy demanding wife, Clare.

Unfortunately Robert E. Lee Fairfield was considered a military prodigy by the Army partly because he was a good intelligent officer and soldier and partly because his mother insisted they were somehow hanging in the family tree of the famous Confederate General Robert E. Lee - thus the name on his birth certificate, Robert Edward Lee Fairfield, proudly placed there by his mother and his one-legged father.

His father lost his limb in Vietnam when, drunk as a skunk, he fell off the third story balcony of a Saigon whore house. The leg, damaged beyond repair, had to come off. The event causing the amputation was written up as a combat incident in order to save the Army embarrassment because the then Major Fairfield was the rich son of somebody who was the rich son of somebody who *was* a rich somebody in Washington politics. They gave him a Silver Star for Valor and soon after recovering with a new phony leg he went to work for the State Department where he did nothing much more than say he worked at the State Department and sign contracts for purchases of pencils and paperclips from some guy in Boston.

Robert E., as he had always been called, was never proud of the name he was given at birth because, as he complained and explained repeatedly to his parents, the original Robert E. Lee lost the war and you simply don't name your children after losers. "Would you," he asked, "have named me *Adolf Hitler Fairfield*?" He was going to change his name but then knowing he was entering the military decided it might actually come in handy. And so with a name like Robert E. Lee Fairfield and a one legged hero father who was the son of the son of somebody, after a stint at Harvard he was destined for a successful military career whether he wanted one or not, and along with such a career came his handpicked wife fresh out of Wellesley College. He didn't want any of this except for the really hot classic 1965 Corvette Stingray sports car that came with the wife. He wanted to be a rock and roll singer and considered himself as well suited and talented to do so as Bruce Springsteen who, in Robert E.'s opinion, had the voice of a crow. The entire situation made him so angry that he wanted to kill someone and he figured the best chance to do that was to join Delta Force, one of the Army's premier fighting and killing groups and the most likely to afford him the quickest opportunity to zap some people and quell his frustrations.

Just as Robert E. curled up to keep from freezing, his cell phone started ringing.

"Oh great. Now you get to go play G.I. Joe and guess who's going to get stuck driving those damn children?"

"Oh, so now they're children?"

"No, they're bad mouthed little turds who know that if I verbally ream their collective asses they can tell Colonel Bitch-Wife Linda and then I'll have to listen to her long drawn out words of wisdom about patience and respect and responsibility and dedication and God, and the entire time in between the lines she is saying to me, '*maintain an even strain or I'll fuck up your life you arrogant Wellesley whore.'*"

"She says that?" asked Robert E. "Why would she say that?"

"Because she only went to Radcliffe College."

"And she actually says that?"

"Yes, with every pore of her body."

"Wow, what a bitch." He snatched up his phone, "Captain Fairfield here." He listened then set the phone down. "I've got to go. Got to be wheels up in thirty-five minutes."

"Thirty-five… What? Wheels up? That means you're going away somewhere. You never go away. You can't go away. It's almost Christmas. Nobody starts a war at Christmas."

"The Japanese did. It was called World War Two. You ever heard of it?"

"But what about *me… ME?* You have any idea what that Colonel Bitch-Wife will do to me if I'm here alone at Christmas. She'll wreak vengeance on me just because I went to Wellesley. I'll be making cookies. I'll be decorating other people's trees. I'll be serving food to needy privates and their families and nasty snotty shitty little kids."

"Is that so bad? Where's your Christmas spirit?"

"And what about driving the kids to school?"

"We don't have any kids."

"Not our kids. We don't have any kids."

"I know that. That's why I said that because I know that."

"I mean those little shits that belong to other officers. That's the whole point; they're not our kids damnit!"

"You want out of the Army so bad then check out an M-4 from the armory. Tell SGT George there that I said it was okay, and then line the little bastards up and shoot'em. Works for me. You can claim temporary insanity or say we have converted to Islam and you were just following the Quran and executing your right to free religion and execution," he suggested as he grabbed his bag and left the house.

"*Me* executing those little bastards?" said Clare to herself as she watched him depart. She then began to wonder if his suggestion was actually possible and if that would be the proper thing for a Wellesley girl to do - except the target she had in mind was the Colonel Bitch-Wife.

It was still pre-dawn forty-five minutes later when Captain Robert E. and eight of his chosen men were armed and in full gear and seated in a military Boeing C-17 Globemaster when the Crew Chief walked by.

"Hey, Chief, what's the hold up? Thought we were supposed to be in the air by now," asked Capt. Robert E..

"Waiting for the Ambassador," answered the Crew Chief.

"Ambassador? What ambassador? What the hell we need an ambassador for?"

"Beats me. Haven't you been briefed?

"Nope. Just got the get-go order and were told it was a hush hush job and we'd be briefed in the air."

"Well then you know more than I do Capt'n. All I know is we're headin' west," said the Crew Chief as he looked to the side door of the aircraft. "Ah, here we go. Last passenger has arrived. I'll tell the aircraft commander we're all set."

Capt. Robert E. looked to the door and in popped a tall hot blonde dressed in camo and loaded for bear. She wore a hip-slinger Beretta, an M-4 assault rifle over her shoulder, night goggles, and an honest to god Rambo knife. She paused, looked around taking in the entire interior of the plane then scanned the Delta boys on both sides until she came to Capt. Robert E., settled her gaze on him for a few seconds and then sat beside him without saying a ward.

Opium, thought Capt. Robert E.. *I'd know that scent anywhere. Opium perfume. Dated a girl at Harvard who used to wear it. I bought her a six ounce bottle once and it cost me a mint. But man was it worth it. Love that scent. Loved that girl,* recalled Robert E.

Ambassador Stella Fulgenze turned and smiled but said nothing. Capt. Robert E. suddenly had a strange feeling. He could swear he could feel her reading his mind and surprisingly he didn't even care. *But if she could,* he thought, *she would definitely be watching and hopefully enjoying an X-rated episode of his memorable Harvard affair.*

"So, we're heading west are we?" he asked.

Ambassador Fulgenzi simply nodded confirmation, but said nothing.

"How far west?" asked Capt. Robert E..

"Yes," she said.

"Yes what?" he asked.

"Yes, it's Opium," she smiled.

Wow, thought Capt. Robert E., *all that and a mind reader to boot. What a package.*

Chapter 18

But Dear Leader – BANG!

"내 Tootsie 롤스가 오래되었습니다! 내 빌어 먹을 토시 롤이 왜 낡은거야?" meaning; "My Tootsie Rolls are stale! Why are my Tootsie Rolls stale?" yelled the North Korean dictator Kim Jong Un. "Who is responsible for this affront to the state? Who? Who are they? Tell me quick and I will shoot a missile at them."

"But Dear Leader, we have no control over them. They come all the way from America after they are imported to Russia and then sold to China and then sold to us. That means sometimes the Tootsie Rolls are, uh, a little aged," replied one of the eight Korean Generals in the room.

"Then why can't we make our own Tootsie Rolls? I want fresh Tootsie Rolls. Why can't we make Tootsie Rolls?"

"Because we have dedicated all of our science efforts to building nuclear missiles so we can blow up America."

"But if we blow up America then we can't get anymore Tootsie Rolls and I want my fuckin' Tootsie Rolls," squealed the Dear Leader.

"Don't know what the big deal is. It's just a little chocolate turd, just like this little turd that thinks he can run our country," whispered one of the generals in the room.

"What? What was that I heard? *A turd*? Did someone call me a turd? Who was it? Tell me, tell me this very instant or I will kill all of you!" yelled and angry Kim Jong Un.

All the Generals in the room, all eight of them, shied away in silence.

"Shit, the chubby little fucker's on a roll today," whispered the same General.

"Ah hah! So it was you General! It was you who offended the Dear Leader!" yelled Kim Jong Un to the wrong general. "Who are you anyway?"

"General Sung Min Park, Dear Leader."

"Why would you say such a thing?" asked Dear Leader Kim Jong Un.

"Please forgive me, Dear Leader, but I do not know of what thing you speak?"

"Yes you do. You know that turd thing."

"What turd thing, Dear Leader?"

"The Tootsie Roll turd thing. Why did you say that Tootsie Roll turd thing and insult the Dear Leader?"

"But Dear Leader, I said nothing."

"Did I say you said this thing?"

"Yes Dear Leader, you said that I said this thing that I did not say but…"

"Enough. Take that man out and shoot him in front of all the troops. Show them that no man, be him a private or a general, may insult the Dear Leader. Do it now, right now! Now, now, now!"

"But Dear Leader, I…"

"Enough! Now where was I?"

"Tootsie Rolls, Dear Leader," said one of the generals as they dragged General Sung Min Park from the room.

"Wow," whispered a general. "I sure got away with that one."

"You!" shouted the Dear Leader. "You the whispering one. Are you not the general who is responsible for my candy?"

"Yes, Dear Leader. I am the one who is honored with the responsibility of maintaining your supply of candy," answered the general. "And, your X-Box and your skateboards and your very, very expensive collection of cars and banana bikes... oh, and the turning ball in your disco room."

"Good. I want fresh Tootsie Rolls. Can you get me fresh Tootsie Rolls?"

"Yes, Dear Leader, on my life I will try to get you fresh Tootsie Rolls."

"You bet your life you will. Might I suggest an idea?"

"Of course, Dear Leader. I welcome your wisdom."

"Then I suggest you call Dennis Rodman and have him fly over here and bring a case of fresh Tootsie Rolls with him. We will shoot some hoops and I might even release one of those American prisoners we have dying in our prisons. Is that a good plan?"

"That's an excellent plan, Dear Leader," replied the general.

"Good. Make it happen. Now my generals, what business do we have today?"

"We are going to shoot another missile," said one of the generals.

"What, again?" said the Dear Leader. "What are we shooting at?"

"At the American Republicans," said another of the generals.

"Are we going to kill the American Republicans?"

"No, Dear Leader," responded one of the generals. "Our missiles aren't actually that good but we say they are so we can shoot at the American Republicans egos and mess with the heads of the Japanese."

"The Japanese?"

"Yes, Dear Leader. We don't like the Japanese because they took our country and raped our women and killed our men and well, other bad things."

"They did that?" asked the Dear Leader.

"Yes, Dear Leader, they did that."

"Why didn't I know this?"

"Um, did not your mother tell you?" asked a general.

"Why would my mother tell me that?"

"Um..." replied a general.

"Well, speak up. Why would she tell me something like that?"

"Um… because your mother is half Japanese," said the general. "Because your mother's mother was raped by a Japanese soldier during the war." Immediately after the general told that to the Dear Leader he closed his eyes and waited.

BANG!

"There will be no more talk of my mother," said the Dear Leader. "Guards, take that man's body out of here."

"Doesn't that little turd realize that a part Jap mom means that he's part Jap too?" mumbled the whispering general.

"Now, what other business do we have to discuss?" said Kim Jong Un as he replaced his gun. "And be quick, I want to finish in time to watch Gilligan's Island."

"The island," said one of the generals.

"Yes," said the Dear Leader. "Gilligan's Island."

"No, Dear Leader. The other island."

"What other island?"

"The one with all the gold and diamonds and oil and uranium."

"Uranium? Isn't that the stuff we need to make big bombs?"

"Yes, Dear Leader."

"Wait a minute. Quick, someone scratch my ass there on the left side right behind my gun."

All seven generals reached out to scratch the Dear Leader's ass which resulted in a full multihanded massage. He wiggled like a happy dog.

"Ahhh yes. Good. Now about that island with that bomb stuff. What about that island? Did we take it? Is it ours?"

"No, Dear Leader, it is not," said one of the generals.

"Why not. I thought we sent a platoon of soldiers to take it for us."

"Yes, Dear Leader, we did," said one of the generals.

"Then why don't we own that island?"

"Uh… because they left," said another one of the generals.

"What do you mean they left? Who left?"

"The platoon of soldiers. They left. They defected."

"What! Defected! A full platoon of North Korean soldiers defected! Where, where did they go?"

"We don't know. They didn't leave a note."

"Damn them! I want you to find them and while you are finding them I want you to find all the members of their families and kill them."

"Yes, Dear Leader."

"Now, did we send more soldiers?"

"Yes, Dear Leader, we did send more soldiers," replied a general.

"Well?"

"Um… they all left, Dear Leader."

"What? You mean they left? Like the other soldiers left? Left left? Like in defected?"

"Yes, Dear Leader. They all left, defected, like the others."

"So, that island isn't ours?"

"No, Dear Leader, the island isn't ours and neither is the gold or diamonds or oil or uranium. It appears it has fallen into other hands."

"Oh well. Can't win them all. Guess we can make bombs without that uranium stuff. We'll just pretend they're real bombs and fool everybody, BUT GET ME SOME FRESH TOOTSIE ROLLS, DAMN IT! CALL DENNIS RODMAN!"

"Yes, Dear Leader," said the six remaining generals in unison.

"By the way, that general I just had killed, he looked familiar."

"Yes, Dear Leader... he was your brother."

"But his name was Park?" said Kim Jong Un."

"Yes, Dear Leader. He was of the five brothers by one of your father's many girlfriends, his bodyguards. I think it was the one that eventually married your uncle that you killed last year."

"Oh, that one. Hmf, oh well. Any other business for today?"

"Yes, Dear Leader. There is the business of the hats," said one of the generals.

"The hats?"

"Yes, Dear Leader. Uh, all the generals would like smaller hats."

"Smaller hats? Why would they want smaller hats? I like the great big round hats. The big hats are bigger than the Russian big round hats and they make our generals look taller. Don't you think they make our generals look taller? And we need our generals to look taller because they are all so short. They need to look taller."

"But, Dear Leader, the other generals around the world are laughing at us and saying we look like Mickey Rooney on a hang glider. And in parades they often have to pin the hats to their heads and that's painful with each goose step."

"Just tell them they need big hats because they have big Korean brains and are smarter than then the rest of the world," said the Dear Leader.

"Yes, Dear Leader, we will tell them that."

"Now is there anything else before I go to watch Gilligan's Island?"

"Just one other thing Dear Leader."

"Well, what is it?"

"The troops, Dear Leader," said a general. "All two million of our troops want to stop goose stepping in our parades. And in fact they want to have to have fewer parades. They don't like goose stepping because they think it looks gay and it hurts."

"Absolutely not," said the Dear Leader. "It looks wonderful and frightens the rest of the world, correct? It frightens the rest of the world because they know a goose stepping army is an army willing to die. They will continue to goose step."

"Bet that fat ass chunky little Tootsie Roll turd couldn't goose step to save his life," said the whispering general.

BANG!

"Anyone else have any comments about my Tootsie Rolls… or my mother?"

"No, Dear Leader," replied the remaining five generals in unison.

"Good. Now somebody call Dennis Rodman and get me some fresh Tootsie Rolls," ordered the Dear Leader. "Oh, and add some Twizzlers to that order as well. Good Twizzlers. Fresh Twizzlers. Oh, and um, some Twinkies. Lots of Twinkies."

"Yes, Dear Leader."

Chapter 19

Big Little Yankee Dude

"Hey there Big Little Yankee Dude!" yelled Tex the Big Bopper. He had just jumped out of his private luxury helicopter after the chopper's landing scattered 500 of his longhorn cattle for miles. No one could hear him because of the noise from the chopper. His ranch hands, thinking the worst of their round up for the day was over, suddenly realized their job had just been totally screwed up by the very man paying them to do the work in the first place and they all looked as though they had just found out there is no Santa Claus.

"Big Little Yankee Dude! Hey BL, where the hell are ya?" yelled Tex.

Over behind the chuck wagon truck sat a couple portolets and, barely audible over the sound of the helicopter and stampeding long horns, could be heard someone inside one of them yelling, "Shut the fuck up!

Can't you see I'm tryin' to take a shit? Jesus Christ, can't a cowboy take a shit in quiet solitude no more?"

"You ain't no damn cowboy you yankee piece a gutter crap so get your funky ass out yonder here where's I can talk at ya," demanded Tex.

The door to the portolet flew open violently and there stood the six foot five inch Big Little Yankee Dude with his hat in hand, jeans down to his boots and his pecker dangling in the prairie breeze. "Who the fuck you callin' gutter crap you little piss ass shitstick! I oughta come over there and land a boot in your gaul damn gonads."

"Well whatever the hell you gonna do, do it quick cause we're headin' out yonder to the Pacific Ocean to do some binness," replied Tex. "But damn it, son, pull up your britches first. I mean, what the hell boy, you tryin' to go *metro* or somp'n?"

"Pacific? What the hell's in the Pacific?" asked Big Little Yankee Dude.

"Water, dumb ass. Loads and loads a water," laughed Tex.

"I don't do water damnit. I do oil... cattle and oil. What the hell you gonna do with a bunch of water?" asked Big Little Yankee Dude as he fixed up his pants and then ruffled his hair before replacing his dirty old sweaty cowboy hat.

"Ain't that kinda binness," said Tex. "More like that job we had years ago down in Veracruz. Maybe even worse."

"Ya don't say?" replied Big Little Yankee Dude. "Then I'm thinkin' maybe I should stop off and pick up my baby. Might come in handy."

"Yep. You might be right there BL so let's get goin'," said Tex as he headed for the chopper.

Big Little Yankee Dude followed while yelling orders to the roundup cowboys, "You boys get them cattle back in. Gaul damn, looky there, ya'll done let'em git scattered all over half a Texas."

The boys looked to the chopper then to the portolet then to the longhorn cattle in the distance. "Sheeeeiiiiit," they all mumbled.

Big Little Yankee Dude's baby was a prized hexagon barrel 3030 Winchester lever action that he took off a Peruvian land pirate 28 years ago when the pirates raided their oil rig down in Argentina. As far as he knew that pirate is still in a shallow grave along with his fellow raiders on a hill just east of the rig and when he was putting them there it seemed ashamed to also put that beautiful inlaid hand carved baby in the ground with its current master. So he decided to give it a new home – in Texas, where he discovered that his new baby never ever missed the target at just about any range.

Big Little Yankee Dude wasn't actually a yankee at all because he was the son of an El Paso south of border dancer and a man from up north who worked the rigs with Tex the Big Bopper's old man. They called him Yankee. When his father, the real yankee dude, got himself killed in an oil rig explosion Tex's father took him in and raised him on the ranch where he and Tex grew up almost as brothers. We say almost because when the old man died he gave everything to Tex except a cool ten million and some stock he gave to Big Little Yankee Dude who, as an adult was still referred to as *Yankee Dude* just as his father was. The Little part of his name came when he was a little greasy kid running around the ranch and the oil rigs. The Big part came when he went off to college to play football where he used to entertain the girls by putting a leather belt around his chest and flexing it with his muscles to snap it apart. He would always end the trick by saying, 'And you should see what I can do in bed.' The name eventually settled to become BL which designated the Big Little part. Only Tex continued to use the Yankee Dude part in that way that an angry mother will use all three names to reprimand her child. There was no prejudice on Tex's part. He simply always treated everyone like shit all the time to maintain his own high leveled ego.

Like Tex, BL was a big man. In fact, he was a few inches taller than Tex and more muscular, which is what got him a free education playing football for the Texas A&M Aggies. Tex was there also but he was too busy messing with women to play ball. Neither of them ever went to class, Big Little Yankee Dude because he was a football star and Tex because his old man had his name on half the buildings on campus. Now he and Tex recall those fun college days by going incognito out on the town looking for fights and women – and they rarely fail. In fact, one time they even took on half the Houston Oilers football team who had come to play the Cowboys and put half of them in the hospital. The two of them thought the experience was lots of fun but the majority of the fans of the team in Houston thought it was a Dallas Cowboys conspiracy. The remaining fans however said that the Oilers were so bad that the missing players weren't even noticed and in fact it may have been an improvement.

Big Little Yankee Dude's primary function now days is to run the Yellow Rose Ranch with an occasional foray to somewhere in the world to sink an oil well.

On the Yellow Rose Corporate private jet, Tex and Big Little Yankee Dude were about to gulp down their third Texas Rye Whiskey when Tex started to fill him in on the situation of the island.

"Okay old man, here's the deal. Seems there's this tiny little island out there in the Pacific, tiny place maybe 25 square miles, ain't even as big as the panhandle on the ranch. Ya see that little geeky lookin' dude sleepin' over there by the bulkhead? Well he's the one discovered it with some computer satellite razzle dazzle. Seems this island is loaded with gold and diamonds and oil and uranium, makin' it one valuable piece of dirt."

"So what's the problem?" asked Big Little Yankee Dude.

"Welp, it seems like ain't nobody owns this precious little piece of paradise and I want it. I want all of it. So's I sent me a team of men there to take it and keep it, but I think those fella's done got into some trouble cause when my little geek Alvin over there was on the radio with'em it sounded like they were bein' tortured or maybe screwed by a bunch of horny pigs. Now I ain't the most sentimental man in all Texas but by gum I ain't one to leave my boys to the enemy where they can be tortured to death. No sir. So's what me and you gonna do is go rescue them boys before they's all done in cause I gotta tell ya, it sounds bad. Sounds like my boys ain't jus' bein' tortured, but they's bein'… do I dare say it… *sexually tortured*."

"Wow, that's bad. Sex should never be torture," said BL.

"No sir'ree, you bet. That there's about as nasty as it gets," Said Tex.

"Sounds like a fun weekend to me. The rescue part I mean." said Big Little Yankee Dude. "By the way, jus' who the hell are the enemy on this island anyway?"

"Now that there is the pickle in the puddin' cause accordin' to what my geek Alvin says, there ain't nobody on that little island except a bunch of horny pigs."

"Pigs?" said Big Little Yankee Dude.

"Pigs," said Tex.

"And you think these pigs are sexually torturin' your team of men? Pigs?"

"Well it could be the Russians or the Chinese or the Jews or the French or the Japanese or North Koreans or the Americans."

"Americans, now that's more believable. I heard plenty about the Americans torturin' folks"

"Oh hell, that's jus' a buncha Democrats blowin' it out their asses. Anybody our boys torture deserves what they git, you ask me. Specially if it's them oil rich ragheads over yonder that keep cuttin' peoples' heads off and shit," said Tex. "Ain't no place for that in the oil binness. Specially when you can afford a perfectly good Smith & Wesson."

"So what we gonna do when we get to that little island?" asked Big Little Yankee Dude. "Sounds like it might be a bit crowded, you ask me. Not that that's sump'n me and baby can't handle. You know baby never disappoints."

"We're gonna do what we do best, BL. We're gonna buy 'em off."

Just then Alvin stirred from his sleep and slowly sat up.

"Hey there tech boy," said Tex. "You ready for another shot a some good ol' Yellow Rose Ranch Texas Rye Whiskey?"

Alvin rolled his eyes in disapproval, fell back into the seat and passed out.

"Hmm... don't know about this millennium bunch now days," said Big Little Yankee Dude. "They's all too damn smart and had too damn much a that kinder gentler Sesame Street shit, you ask me."

"Yep," agreed Tex. "What the hell ever happened to Mighty Mouse. Now that little runt could kick some ass. Better'n Sesame Street."

"Yep," replied Big Little Yankee Dude. "Them millenniums can't hold their liquor. Always protestin' shit. Can't decide what sex they are or who the hell they are on votin' day. Too much Mickey Mouse and not enough Mighty Mouse, you ask me."

"Yep, definitely need more Mighty Mouse… and rye whiskey."

Chapter 20

Lost Ruski

Borris Bolufski squirmed and wiggled and jerked but no matter what he did he just couldn't budge. *It's a good thing,* he thought, *that Vladimir Putin couldn't see him now.*

"I don't like him," said one of the Chinese mercenaries. "He looks like my grandmother who was from Mongolia. You can't imagine how hard it is to imagine a woman who looks like that doing what it takes to make children – and she had eleven of them."

"But what did your grandfather look like?" asked one of the mercenaries.

"You might say he was roughly appealing. Kind of like a good horse."

"Sounds like your grandfather was hung like a horse," said another of the mercenaries.

Borris Bolufski didn't understand a word they were saying which was probably a good thing. He already had a severely feeble sense of self esteem. Getting lost on a small island and stumbling into a group of Chinese mercenaries didn't help. In the situation he was in now he was concerned that if he somehow got out of this situation and had to report to Putin that he had failed his mission he would lose more than what was left of his self esteem. But at the moment he was securely tied to a coconut tree with his own spare change of underwear jammed in his mouth.

"Why don't we just kill him?" one of the Chinese mercenaries asked their commander.

"That's not our mission. We were sent here by Chun-mei Fu Quang to claim this island," replied the commander. "He never said anything about killing people. Just pigs."

"But he's a Russian. Isn't that the same as a pig?"

"So what. We don't kill people just because they are Russian," said the commander.

"Since when?" asked the mercenary.

"Since... uh, the last time we killed Russians," said the commander.

"Chun-mei Fu Quang kills people all the time and he doesn't care who they are. That little queer guy even killed his own parents. So why should we care who we kill?"

"Because."

"Why don't we ask him?" said one of the other mercenaries.

"Ask him what?"

"Ask who?"

"The little Russian man who looks like your grandmother."

"Ask him what?"

"If it's permissible to kill him."

"How can we do that?"

"Lee Wang speaks some Russian. He can ask him."

Lee Wang was stretched out against a tree chewing on a piece of teriyaki chicken.

"Hey Lee Wang, you speak any Russian?"

Lee Wang kept chewing and nodded his head in the affirmative.

"You want to ask this ugly Russian if it is permissible to kill him?"

"Guess so," said Lee Wang. "But it will cost you."

"Oh, here we go again. Every time we ask Lee Wang to do something he wants something in return. You know what Lee Wang… you're a mercenary."

"Yes, I know," said Lee Wang. "But it will still cost you."

"So what do you want for speaking to this Russian in Russian?"

"A picture of your Mongolian grandmother," replied Lee Wang.

"A picture of my grandmother? Are you serious? Why would you want a picture of my grandmother?"

"Because I don't have a picture of my own grandmother so I want to use yours."

"I don't have a picture of my grandmother. I don't even think they have cameras in Mongolia. Do they have cameras in Mongolia?" he asked any of the other Chinese mercenaries. They all shrugged because they didn't know.

"No picture, no Russian," said Lee Wang.

"Why don't we just kill Wang?" asked one of the mercenaries.

"That's not our mission," entered the commander.

"I want to kill the Russian. It won't matter. I don't think anyone will miss him. He's stupid and also ugly like my grandmother and I want to kill him. Besides I'm bored from sitting around watching all those people dancing and singing and having sex and wondering why we can't do that in China."

"Maybe that's why Chun-mei Fu Quang sent us here. I heard he couldn't sell the idea to the government so he decided to do it on his own."

"Could be, but I don't think this is Chun-mei Fu Quang's kind of sex."

They all laughed and then looked again to Lee Wang. Lee Wang gave in, shook his head and conceded to speak to the Russian.

"What's it going to cost us?"

Lee Wang smiled, rose and walked to the very nervous Borris Bolufski. When he yanked the spare tighty-whities out of his mouth, Borris immediately started talking with no intention to stop because he thought for sure that if and when he stopped talking they would kill him. He pleaded for his life and when that got no response he began rattling off everything he knew about the little island and why he was there, trying to convince them he was nothing more than a real estate inspector. He told them about the gold and the diamonds and the oil and even the uranium and as all this spewed out of his mouth, Lee Wang's mouth fell open with astonishment.

"Oh Budda be praised," he said. "Eat your heart out and move over Jackie Chan because we just hit the big time."

"You mean we get to kill him?"

Lee Wang smiled and took a bite of his teriyaki chicken. While chewing he prepared to tell them what he just heard. "I now know why Chun-mei Fu Quang sent us here," said Lee Wang as he swallowed his teriyaki chicken and followed it with a swig of Baijiu. "Aaaaaaaannnd it's going to cost him… *big time*."

Chapter 21

Popo YoYo, Popo YoYo

Within the center of the village's grass huts all the island children had fallen asleep in a circle while playing atop the Black Ass boy's gear. That is all but one being the little girl who was still playing with the radio. She had been sitting there all night fascinated by the little red light that went on and off each time she flipped the toggle switch, and she became even more fascinated when sometimes a voice that sounded a little like Sammytu would come out of the box.

"Sammytu?" she would say.

"What? Sammy what?" the strange voice would sometimes say.

"Bertha Sammytu?" she would say.

"What? Bertha what? Who is this? Who is Bertha? What is Sammytu? Over."

"Over," copied the little girl.

"Over? Over what?" said the voice.

"Over," repeated the little girl.

"What did you say?" said the magic voice from the little box.

"Sammytu Bertha," said the little girl. "Bertha Sammytu."

"WHO THE FUCK IS THIS?" said the voice.

"SAMMYTU. SAMMYTU BERTHA SAMMYTU," replied the little island girl.

"Who the hell is Sammytu?" asked the voice.

"Sammytu funglu," replied the little girl.

"Well fuck you too," said a frustrated techhead Alvin on the other end.

"What? What? Fuck you? Fuck who you?" said an excited Tex the Big Bopper who was sitting nearby listening on his yacht as it plowed through the Pacific toward the little island. "Who you fuckin' on that radio? Where's my Black Ass boys? What the hell's goin' on on that there island?"

"Don't sound like no pig, you ask me," said Big Little Yankee Dude while cleaning his *Lady,* the custom Winchester rifle. "Don't sound like no pig I ever heard, you ask me," he said as he raised another glass of Yellow Rose Texas Rye Whiskey and downed a big gulp, then dipped the cleaning cloth into the Rye Whiskey and used it to wipe off the Winchester.

Just then, on the island, Popo YoYo strolled out of his hut. He always liked to taking walks after his funglu wore off. Popo YoYo spied the little girl playing with the radio and heard the voice coming from inside so out of curiosity he strolled over and sat next to her and listened.

"Sammytu," said the little girl.

"What! Sammy what? Who the hell is this?" came the voice of Tex the Big Bopper.

"Bertha. Sammytu Bertha Sammytu," said the little girl and she began to laugh uncontrollably.

"Bertha! Bertha who? And just what the fuck is so damn funny there Bertha? And where's my boys? What the hell'd you do to my Black Ass boys?"

"Black Ass?" said a surprised Popo YoYo. The mention of Black Ass boys rang a bell in Popo YoYo's mind because they had introduced themselves as such earlier that evening before they were overcome by funglu, so he immediately responded, "Black Ass funglu," he said to the magic box.

"Well fung you too you little island shit. You just wait till I get to that there island. I'm gonna kick your everlastin' ass."

"Shit?" said Popo YoYo. "Shitpot."

"What? What? Are you some kinna smart ass?" yelled Tex.

"Black Ass. Black Ass funglu," said Popo YoYo. "Sammytu funglu."

"Son, when I get done with you, you're gonna wish you was livin' in a igloo some place far away in the south pole."

"North," injected Big Little Yankee Dude.

"What?" asked Tex.

207

"North. Igloos, North Pole," clarified BL.

"Who gives a shit? Got snow down yonder, right?"

"Not igloos. North pole, igloos."

"Yeah yeah," conceded Tex.

"Boy, find out who the hell's talkin' on that damn radio," ordered Tex.

"Calling Black Ass. Come in Black Ass. Over," said Alvin.

"Popo YoYo," said Popo YoYo.

"No, Black Ass. Come in Black Ass, Over."

"Popo YoYo."

"Popo... what? Over."

"Popo YoYo. Popo YoYo," repeated Popo YoYo.

"Popo YoYo?" said Alvin.

"Popo YoYo," repeated Popo YoYo.

"Popo YoYo," repeated Alvin.

"Popo YoYo, Popo YoYo, Popo YoYo," laughed Popo YoYo. Popo YoYo smiled widely and began to laugh because he just heard his name spoken from a small box. Surely, he thought, this small box must be the greatest thing since Hooky's Amazing Big Egg and once he learned to use it he could impress all the islanders and he would become more famous then Hooky ever was. Popo YoYo immediately took action by appointing the little girl as his *Official Fantasy High Priestess* in charge of the *magical small box*. His next course of action was to hide the box in a place where only he and the Official Fantasy High Priestess could find it, then make a law that states if anyone other than he or his Official Fantasy High

Priestess ever touches the magic box they will immediately be denied any funglu for the rest of their life.

"Sammytu," said the newly appointed *Official Fantasy High Priestess*. "Sammytu."

"What? Sammy what?" said Alvin.

"Bertha. Sammytu. Sammytu."

Popo YoYo didn't recognize how the English being spoken on the radio was similar to that spoken by Sammytu possibly because it was garbled Texas slang, but the newly appointed *Official Fantasy High Priestess* recognized it and though it was part of her duty to hide and protect the magic box from all comers, she couldn't wait to have a *show and tell* for Sammytu.

Chapter 22

Force Mageure Suyapa

Secretary General of the United Nations Mr. Ombalega Motoo Wambaga was not one to pass up a lucrative opportunity like the one he had heard about during the recent United Nations assembly. As such, he slipped a little cash to the French Ambassador and found out the exact location of the island and then put his greedy little mind in gear and came up with a plan to snatch the island out from under all the countries that were claiming it.

Wambaga's small country of Suyapa had no military because they didn't need one, and they didn't need one simply because there was always a military presence comprised of UN Peacekeeping Forces. Nor did Suyapa possess a Navy because Suyapa's largest body of water was a manmade lake no larger than twelve square acres that was packed with tourists in paddle boats, crocodiles, and a hippopotamus named Charlie that Wambaga purchased from the San Diego Zoo to add regional color for the tourists. He had to buy the hippo because the entire population of hippos in Suyapa had been wiped out by hunters who paid Wambaga great sums of money for the privilege of shooting one. So now the protected hippo Charlie resides at his country's only resort destination hoping that some day he will get a mate - the favorite destination, by the way, of the UN Peacekeeping Forces, and the only place they could spend their money. He someday hopes to include Rhinoceros or two whenever he can buy for steal them from somewhere. There are none in Suyapa because Wambaga's great white hunters paid to shoot them all.

Wambaga was still trying to crack a deal with Disney to turn his half-ass resort into a mega destination but so far they hadn't come through, claiming the location was too susceptible to being attacked by terrorists, or anyone else with a machete and a grudge. Wambaga was seriously disappointed, especially after he pressured the Nobel Committee on behalf of Disney and NBC to award Obama the Nobel Peace Prize for doing nothing.

Not having an army or navy, Wambaga decided to use the American tactic of approach and accept bids for the job of taking the island for him. As a result he ended up hiring the bidding winners who also were the only bidders and who won the bid by telling other potential bidders and Wambaga they would slaughter their entire families if they were denied the job. So Wambaga's new *force majeure* now consisted of 10 Somali pirates in a leaky old wood hull Desco trawler with so many tar patches that it looked as though it was painted in camouflage.

"I don't understand," said pirate Insharr. "Why we no take the nice boat. I like the nice boat and it don't leak."

"Because," said Afrax the boss pirate.

"Because why because?" asked Insharr.

"Because," said Afrax.

"But the big boat is nice and modern and new and fast. And don't leak so why you say because?"

"Because I say so… and because we gonna sell dat big pretty boat and I don't want no bullet holes to make it cheaper and also because it got blood on da decks and we no clean off dat blood yet. You want to make this trip on a bloody boat with a lot of new bullet holes?"

"This boat bloody and it got bullet holes. That why it leak," said Insharr.

The other eight pirates all shook their heads in agreement with Insharr. They didn't want to sell the nice boat; they wanted to enjoy the great big boat they took from that rich British guy who they sold for ransom six weeks ago for a million US Dollars they used to buy new guns. And the big pretty boat has a nice sound system and satellite TV with the Playboy Channel. They didn't like using the old boat because they knew the American Navy could catch them and shoot them if they used a slow boat. Besides, the new boat had a toilet that worked all the time and the old Desco trawler's toilet was always clogged and they had to hang their asses over the side to take a shit.

The boss pirate, Afrax Absimil, didn't like what he was hearing. To him it was starting to sound like a possible mutiny and one thing he didn't put up with was any mutinous attitudes by his pirates. His remedy was simple.

"Hey Insharr," he called from his place at the wheel.

Insharr, who was thinking about how in two minutes he would have to hang his ass over the side to take a shit, turned and said, "What?"

Afrax shot him.

"Now you done it," said pirate Kaafiye.

"Done what?" asked Afrax.

"Now you got more blood on the deck. And Insharr owed me twenty dollar."

"Forget your twenty dollar and throw him overboard and water the deck," ordered Afrax.

"But you didn't want no blood on the deck," questioned Kaafiye.

"I no want no new blood on the big new boat deck. I no care about dis boat cause it already all bloody."

"But that not people blood. That fish blood."

"Blood is blood. What the difference?" said Afrax.

"I think we should get rid of dis boat and get a boat that don't leak and the shitter works all da time," said Kaafiye.

"Maybe you want to be some new blood on dis boat?" said Afrax.

"No," replied Kaafiye, "I juz don't wanna have ta hang my ass over da side to take a shit. You remember little Fowsi. He hung his ass over the side and fell off and den got all chopped up under da boat and da sharks eat him."

"Throw Insharr to the fishes and water dat blood. I da Captain now and you do what I say."

"You only been da Captain for two days. How come you da Captain anyhow?"

"Because I kill da udder Captain because he no wanna sell da big pretty boat. What you care? You gonna make a bunch a money on dis job anyhow?" said Afrax.

"I still no like dis boat and I not sure you know where we going," said Kaafiye.

"I not need to know cause dis ting on da boat know where we goin. Wambaga's man, he put dis ting on here and he say all we gotta do is go where it say go. Dat's how I know where we goin', so there. Now, you wanna be some new people blood on da deck or what?"

"I no like dat Wambaga man. I tink he a big fat liar," said Kaafiye.

"We no have to like him. He got lotsa money. He even say he gonna buy the big pretty boat after we clean off all da blood so he can go to da island we gonna get for him. So you see, dats a good deal and dats why I da Captain now."

"I tink he fulla camel shit and I bet he no gonna hang his ass over da side to dump any of it."

"Shut up and throw Insharr over the side."

"I gonna throw Insharr over da side but I no gonna wash none a his blood," defied Kaafiye.

"I no care if you do or if you don't. But if I step on his blood and fall down and brake my head... den I gonna shoot you."

"Okay, I gonna wash da blood."

Chapter 23

Merry Funglu One and All

"Hey Corky, isn't today Christmas?" asked Herpie.

"Don't know. Could be," replied Corky as he flopped buck-ass naked backward into the surf. "You know, this place isn't half bad. Good food, good people, warm sunshine all the time, and that funglu stuff, wow man, just think if we could bottle that shit."

"Yeah," said Herpie. "And wow what a night last night. I'll be honest; I didn't think I had it in me. Must be something super in that funglu shit because it sure as hell got my ticker tuned up." Herpie flopped down next to Corky. He then stood in waist high water and pretended to be riding a surfboard. "Wooooo, bitchin' waves here duuuude. Like awesome pipeline, duuude," he laughed.

"Me to," said Chow Chow as he waddled from the beach into the surf next to them. He adjusted his fanny pack which kept floating up and revealing his nuts. "Thata funglu'a stuff dun gotta my rigatoni on'a the rise'a. And's den them ladies started foolin' around'a and well... next'a ting ya know I was'a doin' da doodle all night."

"Yep, that sounds about right," agreed Herpie. "Same with me and I gotta tell ya I ain't had a night that good for a few years now. And of course having herpes and all don't help any. Always in the back of your mind, ya know? Kind of sidetracks your ambitions, ya know?"

"Herpie... uh, I got something to tell you and, uh... well I guess this is as good a time as ever," said Corky as he swished around in the surf.

"What? You tellin'a me that chew gots da herpes?" said an exited Chow Chow to Herpie. "Dun'a you know dat'a you gonna get everybody on dis island with them herpies?"

"Herpie... um, I got something to tell you and I'm thinking this is as good a time as ever to do it," said Corky as he looked down into the water to avoid Herpie's eyes.

Herpie turned to Corky, "Oh no. Don't tell me you're dying. I don't think I could take it. Not after losing Samson. No, I can't take losing two friends in one week."

"No dumb ass, I'm not dying. At least I don't think so," said Corky.

"Yeah, if he gots da herpes den'a he's a pretty much dumb ass okay," entered Chow Chow. "He gonna infect everybody on'a da island. And here I'm'a just'a changed from a boys man to a girls man because of'a dat funglu stuff."

"What I want to tell you Herpie, is, well... you remember years ago when you went to the doctor and found out that you had herpes?"

"Yeah, sure. How could I forget," said Herpie.

"Well, you see, um... that doctor wasn't actually a doctor."

"What? What do you mean he wasn't a doctor?"

"He was... uh, he was a Three Horses Beer salesman."

"Well then how the hell did he know I have herpes?" asked Herpie.

"Um, he didn't."

"What?" said Herpie.

"What?" said Chow Chow just as a wave knocked him down and under.

"He didn't know. He wouldn't know a case of herpes from a case of beer. He was a fraud, a beer salesman," said Corky.

"A fraud?"

"A frog?" said Chow Chow as he bobbed out of the water. "He gots some kind'a frog herpes?"

"Yeah, a fraud," said Corky, uncomfortably. "Not a frog, Chow Chow. A fraud. A beer salesman."

"Chew mean da beer guy, him gotta da herpes, too?"

"Why would he claim to be a doctor? Why would he say I had herpes? Why would he do that? I know I didn't understand a word he said but you and Crazy Bob said that he said that I had herpes. If he didn't say that then what the hell did he say?" asked Herpie.

"He was explaining why Three Horses Beer makes you piss a lot. He thought that's what you wanted to know because you kept pointing at your dick. He didn't know shit about herpes, never heard of it. He was a Three Horses Beer salesman," said Corky.

"Why did you guys tell me that?"

"Yeah," said Chow Chow. "Why you guys say dat?"

"Because that's what men do, Chow Chow. It's things like that that make me kick their asses," said Slammin' Sammy as she strolled up to the group in the surf.

They all paused as Slammin' Sammy's fabulous wet body moved closer. For a moment Herpie lost all thought as he focused on her incredible breast until he was shoved by Corky. Then Corky became distracted for the same reason until Chow Chow interrupted.

"Hey man, you don't wanna stare too long or she'a gonna punch your eyes out."

"Uh... oh yeah," said Corky as he turned back to Herpie. "It was a joke, Herpie. You never had herpies, all you had was the drip and we cured that with Three Horses Beer because Three Horses Beer cures everything. But you were so upset thinking you had incurable herpes that we couldn't bring ourselves to tell you the truth, and then the longer it went on the funnier it got and then we started calling you Herpie and one thing led to another and, well... you know."

"No I don't know. I've been carrying guilt around for forty years thinking I contaminated the entire island of Madagascar with herpes." Herpie paused and thought a moment. "You know what? Come to think about it, I never got a complaint by any Madagascar women. Well, there was that woman from Belgium but she was complaining about something else."

"That's okay, Herpie. I don't think Madagascar needs any help. They're well capable of contaminating themselves. Besides, if you think about it, it made you a better, more thoughtful man."

"You think so?"

"You know what they say, Herpie – what doesn't kill you makes you stronger," said Slammin' Sammy.

"It didn't kill me. Well, I mean, it couldn't kill me because I didn't have it, but… I think I'm going to kill someone else."

"Are you sure because remember, it made you a more thoughtful man. I believe that. Sure I do," said Corky.

"A better man, a more thoughtful man?"

"Yep."

"Then you won't feel so bad when I kill you?" said Herpie.

"Why would you want to kill me?"

"Because you put me through forty years of grief and worry."

"Oh, that's bad. I think I might kill somebody for that," said Slammin' Sammy.

"Dats'a right," said Chow Chow.

"But now you're a better more thoughtful man," repeated Corky.

"I still want to kill you… for what you did."

"You can't kill me. You said you can't lose two friends in one week, but you *can* kill Crazy Bob. It was all his idea anyway."

Herpie sat down on the sandy bottom of the shallow water and hung his head. When he looked up he was staring at an incredible set of beautiful tits that took his head and pulled it to them for comfort. Herpie wondered what he would have to do to savor the moment with Slammin' Sammy's boobs for the rest of eternity.

"Now, now, Herpie, remember you are a better, stronger man than you ever were before and we are all with you," said Slammin' Sammy.

"Forty years and all that time...I thought I had..." he mumbled into her boobs. He then looked up with a smile. "Do you know what that means? It means I can funglu on this island everyday and not worry about contaminating the population. Man, that's better than any of that damn gold and diamonds and oil and shit. What good is all that at our age anyway. Hell, this place is heaven on earth, Corky. We should just stay here for the rest of our lives... what's left of our lives."

Corky smiled, "I think you got something there, *Mister Better Thoughtful Herpie.*"

"He certainly does," said Slammin' Sammy as she washed the water over her shoulders.

"You bet your boobs... um, I mean, you bet you're a... your bottom... uh, bottom dollar," agreed Herpie.

"Hey you guys," came a voice from the beach.

They looked up to find MacDugal standing with a smiling girl under each arm.

"Hey mates, ain't today Christmas?"

"Not sure," replied Corky. "Could have been yesterday or tomorrow or next week. I quit keeping track about ten years ago. Makes me homesick."

"I don't have herpes," said Herpie.

"Yeah, I know," said MacDugal.

"Does everybody know?" Herpie asked Corky.

"Of course," said Corky.

"Then why did you guys keep that record of my, um… social life?"

"Oh, you knew about that?" asked MacDugal.

"Sure I knew. Why wouldn't I know? So, why'd you guys do that?" asked Herpie.

"Oh, just for shits and giggles, you know," said MacDugal. "We really didn't care what you did with your pecker, mate, but it was somethin' to do. Can't just drink Three Horses Beer and play pool and darts and tell war stories all the time. Need a little stimulus on occasion, right mate? You know, a little mental challenge now and again. Well, I'll be a wallaby's ass, will ya take a look at that sunset?"

They all turned to look at the sunset while MacDugal studied Slammin' Sammy's ass and filled his head with wishful thinking.

"I think I'm going to kill you," said Herpie as he turned back around.

"Oh listen, mate. Ya think you can wait til after Christmas? There's a bunch of little kids here that ain't never heard of Christmas and I think it should be our mission to bring it to 'em."

"Okay, deal," said Herpie. "But I might kill you after New Years."

"Quite all right there, mate. We's good with that. But not until after the holiday. Don't wanna mess up anybody's Christmas, right mate?"

"Okay then. So who's going to be Santa Claus?" asked Corky.

"Well, I got that covered. Thinkin' maybe T-Bone might fit the bill. He's a lot rounder than the rest of us, but I ain't so sure hows I'm gonna come up with the six white boomers."

"The what? What the hell are boomers?" asked Herpie.

"I believe he's talking about kangaroos," said Slammin' Sammy. "You know I fought one of those critters once in Brisbane."

"Dat'sa right," confirmed Chow Chow. "And she kick'a dat big rabbits ass."

"Roos, mate. The six white kangaroos that pulls ol' Saint Nick's sleigh. And the dingo that leads them all. Sometimes I think you yanks don't know shit."

They all stood silent for a long moment and stared at MacDugal.

"Are those tits real?" MacDugal asked of Slammin' Sammy.

"I don't think I'll wait until new years. I think I'll kill him now," said Herpie to Corky.

"Okay," said Corky.

"I think I might help you," said Slammin' Sammy.

"Uh oh," said Chow Chow.

"What's wrong, Chow Chow," asked Corky.

"I lost my fanny pack," replied Chow Chow.

"I don't think you really need it, do you?" asked Herpie.

Chow Chow stood up in the shallow water and began searching for his fanny pack. When the others saw him they all agreed it should be found.

"I think we better find his fanny pack before the men in the village decide to roast his ass," said Corky.

"Why would he want to hide that thing? If it was mine I'd hang a bell on it and take appointments," said Herpie. "Wow, and to think it belongs to a midget."

Chapter 24

Helta Skelta Delta

Captain Robert E. and his eight man Delta Force team along with Ambassador Stella Fulgenze went to work immediately after being dropped off on the aircraft carrier, U.S.S Abraham Lincoln. They were met by a SEAL team that had been prepping for two days to assault the island. The SEAL team was then told to stand down by Ambassador Fulgenze. When they objected, claiming they were under orders from the Secretary of Defense the Ambassador said coldly, "You will stand down or I will put you and that fucking Admiral Dickhead in a low hole at Gitmo. If you don't like it, call the man at Pennsylvania Avenue for confirmation."

"Yes ma'am, I believe I will do just that," replied the team leader.

"And I believe you will not, Captain. Now get your boys out of this prep area and let these people do their jobs," said an authoritative voice from across the hanger deck. They all turned and saw it was Fleet Commander Admiral John Paul Bates, and without a word the SEALs departed the area.

"Sorry, ma'am, those boys aren't used to taking shit from a woman, especially one from Washington," said Admiral Bates.

"And what about you, Admiral. You like taking shit from a female from Washington?"asked the Ambassador.

"No ma'am, not at all. I've got years of practice doing just that. You see, my wife is from Washington," smiled the Admiral. "But I got to tell you, it's easier running this fleet than dealing with that woman."

"Captain, you have a bird that can drop my guys high over that little island?" asked the Ambassador.

"Bet your ass I do, ma'am."

"Good. Then get it prepped because we'll need it for a high level HALO."

The Admiral stared for a moment, then saluted and said, "Yes ma'am. You want fries with that?"

"You want your ass kicked," replied the Ambassador.

Admiral Bates wasn't quite sure what to make of this bitch boss from DC, but he was sure of his orders which instructed him to give her and her crew anything and everything they wanted without question or delay.

"Oh, and don't forget to tell your SEALs thanks for the use of their jump gear," she added coldly.

Captain Robert E. watched with amazement at how easily the Ambassador manipulated men and just about anyone else when she wanted or needed something. He liked it because she was the opposite of his nagging whiny wife Clare, and if there was one thing he really liked it was an independent decisive woman.

His men looked about with sly smiles of approval and one, a Sergeant Jack Forester, spoke up and asked, "Are we to assume that you're going to make a high altitude jump with us, ma'am, a HALO jump? Pretty damn tricky and dangerous. You trained for it.?"

"Captain Fairfield, am I to assume that you and your boys expect me to qualify my presence on this op?"

"Uh... no ma'am. What would give you that idea?" replied Captain Robert E.

"Good. That's very good. Because I would hate to put one of your fucking boy scouts on his ass and out of commission just to demonstrate my qualifications."

"Yes ma'am, I understand," said Captain Robert E. while looking to his boys with a disciplinary nod. He then turned back to the Ambassador and asked, "By the way Ambassador, I was wondering if and when you intend to share the plan of attack with us and maybe even tell us what our objective happens to be... in other words, why the hell we're here?"

"Okay, Captain, you're right. Now's the time." She turned and faced the rest of the Delta team. "Listen up people. Our plan is a simple one. There is a small island out there in the ocean, I say small being from 20 to 25 square miles, and it is highly valuable and essential to our government. We, meaning you, are going to drop on that piece of rock, take it, claim it, and hold it."

"That's it?" said Sergeant Forester. "We're just going to jump down there at night without any intel? What are we up against? Who we going to have to fight? What's the terrain? Christ sakes lady, we're good but we're not psychic... or stupid."

All went silent for a long moment as everyone fully expected lightning to flash from the Ambassador's eyes right through Forester's head. Following a long silent moment the Ambassador finally decided to come clean. All of the team watched intently as she tossed her gear over her shoulder.

"Pigs," said the Ambassador.

"What?" said Sergeant Forester.

"Pigs," repeated the Ambassador. "The island is occupied by some horny pigs. And to the best of my knowledge they are not trained and are not armed."

"So what you're saying is," said team member Sergeant Nino Bambino, the resident clown of the team, "if we don't first get killed making a night HALO jump into unknown terrain we face the horrendous risk of possibly getting raped by some horny pigs?"

"Yes," said the Ambassador.

"Pigs?" said Capt. Robert E.

"Or..."

"Or what?" asked Sergeant Bambino.

"Or maybe some Russians or... some Chinese or... some Jews or... some Texans or..."

"Or? There's more *or's*?" asked Capt. Robert E.

"Or… who knows, or maybe all of the above," concluded the Ambassador. "But don't worry. Worst case scenario is we'll be roasting a pig for lunch with… maybe some coconuts or something," said the Ambassador.

The Delta boys all stood and stared. Never had they been asked or ordered to go into an operation blind with no intel, and they pretty much began to think that everybody in Washington was an idiot. Who knows, maybe they're correct.

"Okay dammit," said the Ambassador. "As the late great Johnny Unitas used to say in the locker room before the game, *'Talk is cheap, let's play ball.'* Now grab your shit and let's get wheels up… so we can get down and dirty on that island."

With that said the Delta team came around and jumped to her orders because as everyone knows all macho combat guys (and low IQ NFL players) always respond to football colloquialisms, especially if they are sourced by or include someone like the late greats Johnny Unitas, Jim Brown, or Bear Bryant.

Capt. Robert E. was a great football fan but he was more of a Patriots and Tom Brady guy and actually didn't know much about Johnny Unitas who was before his time, so his thoughts shifted over to the *I hate the Army* section of his brain and he suddenly realized that the promising career that he didn't want in the first place just graduated him from finding missing little rat dogs named *Consti* at Camp David to fighting *horny pigs* on an

obscure island in the middle of the Pacific. On the bright
side, he should be a well qualified animal control officer
as a civilian. Like all wars in which his family has been
involved, he had no clue as to what, where, or why this
one was taking place so he just kicked back and let his
mind wonder to how he would improve the music of
Bruce Springsteen.

The Delta contingent was now camped out on deck
waiting to board their aircraft when they started to kill
time with conversation.

"Hey, Forester," said Sgt. Nino Bambino. "I ever tell
you about the time we were jumpin' HALO over Serbia
on Christmas Eve back in '09?"

"Nope," answered Sgt. Forester.

"Well now there we were divin' outta this plane at
high altitude in the pitch black of night and I'm free-
fallin' faster than shit through a goose when all of a
sudden in the distance I see there's something with red
lights coming right at me. And I mean that sucker is
coming on like an F-18 on after burners. I mean it was
coming on fast man, and I ain't had no time at all to get
out of the way so all I could think of was to pull my chute
which I'm worried would catch the wind and throw me
way off course from the rendezvous with the team. Welp,
it was live or die, so in a major panic I closed my eyes
and pulled the cord and out pops my chute but…! and I
mean this is a big *BUT*. That thing flew past me so fast
that it drafted my chute and twisted it up like a girl in the
back seat on prom night. And would you believe my

reserve chute jammed and the next thing I know I'm in the free-fall of death, but… and I mean this is another big *BUT*… that thing that flew past me turned right around and came back and I'm thinking, *that son of a bitch is coming to finish me off*, but…"

"Jesus Christ Bambino, will you quit with the buts already and get on with the story," said Sgt. Forester.

"Okay, okay," said Sgt. Bambino. "So this thing turns around quicker than any plane I ever saw and comes right at me and then just as easy as if it's a sunfish sail boat it slows down and slides under and catches me, just as easy as you please."

"Catches you? What you mean it *catches* you?"

"You know, it just pulled up under me and caught me all nice and safe like."

"Shit Bambino, that's a load of crap," said Sgt. Forester.

"Nope, I'm telling you it's not a load of crap. And you know who it was? It was none other than… Santa Claus himself and his reindeer and I got to tell you, that sucker can really fly and that old bastard was laughing all the way."

"Captain, I'm thinking it might be time for Bambino to retire. I think the stress from not having enough post traumatic stress is stressing him out and he's become an ineffective soldier and an obstacle to the success of our mission – whatever the fuck that is. And that damn WOP takes too long to tell his lies."

"Hey, who you callin' a WOP, nigger," said Bambino. "I'll have you know I'm half Irish."

"Yeah, and I'm half Martian, *meatball*."

"Martian? I'll be damned. You know I think I dated your sister once," said Bambino.

"Looks like some hinky weather out there, Captain. Don't think it's gonna get any better either," said Sgt. Hannity. "Looks like it could be a rough ride by tonight."

"Not my call, Hannity. Up to the lady," replied Captain Robert E.

"That was a bullshit story, Bambino," said Sgt. Forester.

"It was a good story. Just his way of saying 'Merry Christmas', Forester," said Captain Robert E. with a smile. He turned to the Ambassador, "No problem ma'am. Does this bother you? Because these guys do this sort of thing all the time. Helps cut the tension," he said as he tried to remember just how much tension existed, if any, when they were searching for the President's dog, Consti.

"Not at all Captain. But I'm wondering... do they know which end the bullets come out or should I give them a lesson or two?"

"Is it Christmas? I'm not sure because we've hopped through a couple of time zones since we left home. So if it's Christmas back home it's not Christmas here, or not yet, or is it over back there or what," asked Sgt. Forester.

"Ask Asher. He's taking the time hacks," said Captain Robert E.

"Hell, Captain, Asher's Jewish. He doesn't give a shit about Christmas."

"Sure he does. His old man imports more Christmas shit from China, Korea, and Mexico than Wal-Mart. How you think he got that bad-ass Jaguar?" said Capt. Robert E. "I'd say that gives him a pretty good reason to care, right Asher?"

"Bet your ass, Cap'n," replied Asher. "I care all the way to the bank. And by the way, yeah, today is Christmas in this particular time zone and what the hell do you care, Forester? Aren't you one of those Kwanzaa dudes thinks all us white folks got their holidays so you invented your own."

"No, not really, I'm a Buddhist. Born a Buddhist. Always been a Buddhist."

"Then you don't celebrate Christmas?" ask Bambino.

"Sure we do. We just don't buy out Toys-R-Us when we do. We keep it lean is all, you know, no flat screen TVs or Cadillacs."

"No Caddies. Wow, that must make it hard to live with the neighbors, huh?" said Bambino. "And if you're a Buddhist then what the hell you doin' in this business?"

"I'm here to give you a hard time, Bambino. Captain, I think that Dago needs a lobotomy," said Forester. "A few too many anchovies floatin' around that brain of his… if he's got a brain."

"I'll see what I can do when we get back," said Captain Robert E.

"Appreciate that Captain," said Forester with a smile.

"Happy belated Hanukkah there Asher," Said Captain Robert E.

"Thanks, sir. And a Merry Christmas to one and all... even you Bambino."

"Hey, anybody have any favorite Christmas songs we can sing?" asked Bambino.

"Uh, White Christmas," said Forester. "I'm a New Yorker and I like a good white Christmas."

"Nah, I like Trop Rock. I'm a Floridian," said Sgt. Leroy Cross."

"Trop Rock. What the hell's *Trop Rock*?" asked Forester.

"You know, like, Trop Rock is Tropical Rock like Jimmy Buffett. And I like his song *Christmas Island*."

"Oh," said Sgt. Forester.

"How 'bout you Ambassador? Got any favorite Christmas songs?" asked Sergeant Bambino.

"Fuck you," said Ambassador Stella Fulgenzi.

All the Delta guys went silent.

Captain Robert E. looked to the Ambassador and said, "You don't have a lot of friends, do you?"

Chapter 25

 Mayday! Mayday!

Tarabi hung over the side of the boat regurgitating his corn meal and beans. It appeared he had reached the point where if he continued he would eventually begin heaving up his inner organs. Tarabi was the youngest pirate of the group. He had been forced into the business by his father who wanted the rewards of the profession but was too busy with his own occupation as a radical Muslim terrorist killing infidels to do it himself, and too lazy, so he farmed out his son Tarabi.

Afrax Absimil looked out of the bridge and asked, "What wrong with Tarabi? He sure no look like he takin' a shit."

"He pukin'," replied Sharmarke.

"I know he pukin'. How come he pukin'?" said Afrax.

"He pukin' because he been down below breathin' all dat fumes and stuff," said Sharmarke.

"Den why he stay down dare? Why he not come up here where we got good air?"

"He can't," said Sharmarke.

"Why not?"

"Because Tarabi da pump man and da pump man always down below because da pump is down below."

"No it not. Da pump got a switch up here, see. You turn on da switch and it pump out da water," said Afrax as he turned on the switch.

"Not no more," said Sharmarke. "Da pump not pumpin' no more so Tarabi become da pump man on da hand pump because he da new guy and da knew guy always da pump man and it makin' him sick."

"So make Tarabi come topside," said Afrax.

"Den who gonna be down below?"

"Nobody. I don't want nobody gettin' sick like Tarabi, so nobody go down below," said Afrax.

"Okay, but den we gonna sink," said Sharmarke.

"What you mean we gonna sink? Why we gonna sink?"

"Because da boat got bullet holes and da water comin' in and if we no get da water outta da boat it gonna sink. Dat why we gonna sink."

"Den go fix da bullet holes," said Afrax.

"We did fix da holes but no good cause da holes still be leakin," said Sharmarke. "Dis a old slow boat. We coulda used dat nice new big boat with the music and TV and a good shitter but now we gonna be sinkin'."

"Den I guess we gonna have to put Tarabi back down below," said Afrax. "You know… because he da new guy."

"Tarabi can't no go below no more. Tarabi can hardly walk no more," said Sharmarke.

"Why he can no walk no more? He fall down in some people blood?"

"No. He sicker den a drunk monkey," said Sharmarke. "Dats why."

"Den what we gonna do?" asked Afrax.

"You da Captain now. Dat what you say. You say, *I da Captain now and you do what I say,* cause you kill da udder boss cause he don't wanna sell da udder boat. So now we on da old boat and we gonna sink. So okay, you da new boss so what you gonna say we do?"

Just then Tarabi looked up onto the horizon and spied another boat. "Hey boss!" he yelled just before he heaved again. "Blaaaaahhhhg. Hey… blaaahhg. I see boat!" he pointed. "BLAAAAHHHG!"

Sharmarke looked out, then grabbed the binoculars and studied the boat. "Ooooh, hey boss. That a real nice big boat out dere. I tink dat boat even nicer den our new big boat back home. And dat big boat even got a nudder boat on top of da big boat. I bet it got tree maybe four good shitters too."

"Let me see," said Afrax as he pulled the binoculars away from Sharmarke. "Hmm, I tink maybe you be right. I tink maybe we gonna need dat big boat."

"Because dis old boat be sinkin'?" said Sharmarke.

"No," replied Afrax. "Because it got good shitters."

"Ahhhh, now you bein' a good boss, boss."

The big new boat in the distance was none other than the *Yellow Rose*, the official yacht of the Texas Yellow Rose Corporation and one of Tex the Big Bopper's toys - part of a collection of planes, choppers, boats, cars, guns, rye whiskey, politicians, and women.

"I jus' don't git it," said Big Little Yankee Dude. "You got everthang any man would want. So what the hell you want with a piece a little shit island like that? Well, I mean, 'sides from all the money you'd be makin' that you don't even need, hell you don't even eat pig bar-b-que. Don't make no sense, you ask me. Why don't you jus' kick back and go fishin' or somethin'?"

"Tried that once. Killed me a fourteen foot great white shark off the coast of South Africa once. Then when I got home a whole buncha them tree huggin' nature lovin' dorks started demonstratin' in front of my office buildin' sayin' I was destroyin' nature and all that kinda shit. I tried tellin' em that I was jus' makin' it safer for their little toddlers to play in the ocean but they's a stubborn buncha piss ants and jus' as bothersome."

"Don't believe I heard about that one. Well whatcha do about em?"

"Well, when talkin' didn't work I called on my two assistants, Mr. Smith and Mr. Wesson. Couple pops in the air and those little unemployed scuzzbuckets scattered like roaches. Except for this one stubborn girl kept standin' there tellin' me I was a destroyer of the planet and shit. She was a bit of a looker too sos' I took her inside to get an education about what we actually do, then I screwed her brains out, gave her a new Mustang car and ten thousand bucks and sent her on her way. Last I heard she was makin' rock and roll videos and save the armadillo documentaries and shit."

"Yep, nothin' like a little diplomacy you ask me," said Big Little Yankee Dude. "But some a them little people jus' never learn, you ask me."

As they lay in the boat's cushioned deck lounges sucking on Texas rye whisky, listening to Hank Williams classics, and talking of old times, they kept their eyes on an old boat in the distance.

"You been out yonder cowboyin' sos' I'm guessin' your eyes are a whole bunch better'n mine, sos' tell me somthin' BL," said Tex.

"Okay, whatcha wanta know thar Tex?" said BL.

"I wanna know does that there boat out yonder look like it's sinkin'?"

Big Little Yankee Dude focused and studied the old boat on the horizon for a good while and finally said, "Yep."

A few minutes later the Captain of the Yellow Rose came to Tex and informed him, "Sir, I thought it prudent to inform you that we are receiving a *mayday* call from another vessel."

"Mayday? Hell, it's December, Captain," said Tex.

"A mayday call is a distress signal, sir. It's coming from that old boat out there on the horizon. We're the closest to the vessel and according to their distress call… they're sinking."

"Sinkin'?"

"Yes, sir. Sinking. With nine souls on board."

"They tell you all that with a mayday?"

"Yes sir."

"Must be foreigners if they don't know what month it is. Or maybe they been out here a long time," speculated Tex. "Well now, I really wasn't countin' on any other passengers on this here trip. Got some serious binness going on."

"Um, sir, Maritime law and the common law of the sea dictates that…"

"Yep, I get it, Captain. What say we go see what we can do for those poor fuckers… and tell the cook we might be havin' comp'ny for dinner and he might have ta cook up some kinda foreign shit."

"Yes sir."

"Looks like a workin' man's boat. Might be some good ole boys. Good ol' boys might come in handy on that thar island yer so hot for. Never know. Could be some serious dangerous pigs on that thar island. Some good ol' boys might come in handy. Might be some good pig killers there," Big Little Yankee Dude snickered.

"Nah, don't need no good ol' boy pig stickers," said Tex.

"Why not?" asked Big Little Yankee Dude.

"Cause I got you," laughed Tex. "And you got… the *Winchester Lady*."

"Sheeeeiiiiiiit," said Big Little Yankee Dude.

"Sheeeeiiiit," said Tex.

Chapter 26

Ho Ho Popo YoYo

The Black Ass boys had all the islanders assembled in the village square with the children clustered in the front. Opposite, they had erected from bamboo and palm fronds between two huts a type of entertainment stage lit with a surround of tiki torches. The Australian MacDugal had taken charge and was acting as director of what he announced (with the help of Sammytu) to be the First Annual Whatchamacalit Island Christmas Pageant, complete with Santa Claus and his six Roos.

The children all perked up when suddenly from behind the stage came the sound of ten members of Team Black Ass singing *We Wish You a Merry Christmas*. While they were singing there came from the back of the stage, director, producer, and all around talent scout, one Duffy MacDugal, who tried his best to announce the show above the over-volume bad voices of the Black Ass Bar Chorus. They were singing loud and it seemed the further along they progressed through the song, the faster they sang. One would think it was from enthusiasm, but the truth was they had each just downed a swig of funglu spiked coconut milk and it was starting to kick in. They didn't pretend to be good singers and the only singing practice they'd had since Vietnam was, We *Gotta Get Out of this Place*, after at least five Three Horses Beers as well as the theme song *North to Alaska* from the John Wayne movie, North to Alaska, and a medley of the Beatles songs from the album, Sergeant Pepper's Lonely Hearts Club Band. One of them did know the Marine Corps hymn but he would never sing it because it made him feel guilty and he was always afraid someone would ask him where the halls of Montezuma were and why were the Marines there in the first place. Questions that always came up but none of which he or most other Marines knew the answers.

So the islanders got their first taste of western entertainment consisting of *We Wish You a Merry Christmas* with *North To Alaska* tacked on to the end of the song because, said MacDugal, 'it snows in Alaska.' During the songs two of the little island girls attempted to dance around on stage with two very large bows made of palm fronds. After the musical introduction came the story of Christmas (according to Duffy MacDugal) that included Aborigines, kangaroos, and a dingo named Roger. MacDugal had recruited a few islanders to act in this part of the show and as he told the story, which none of the islanders understood except Sammytu who was interpreting to the others and getting it all wrong, the volunteer actors would parade across the stage with straw hats and covered in grass and palm frond Christmas bows with a small torch looking stupid. Crazy Bob thought they all looked like bad imitations of the Statue of Liberty but he wasn't going to argue with MacDugal because he really didn't want to get involved in the event any more than he already was and, he thought, how do you argue anything about Christmas with a guy who claims Santa's sled is pulled by Roger the dingo and six kangaroos?

Hiding in the nearby brush crouched the team of Chinese mercenaries who were completely engrossed with what they were seeing, not so much because of the content of MacDugal's production but because many of his actors were buck ass naked pretty girls. MacDugal always did have a good eye for pretty women and, of course, he picked the best on the island for his show. As far as Christmas was concerned, to the Chinese it was just some stupid thing that happens in America every year and a way for all their cousins to make a lot of money. So the mercenaries sat and they watched and they drooled and they fantasized all through the show, and every once in a while one of them would slip up and applaud but quickly catch himself after his hands came together for a single clap and the others would snatch up their weapons, point them at his head and kick him for being so stupid.

On the second occasion when one of the Chinese clapped it was noticed by only one person in the entire village. She watched the bushes from where the sound came and then reverted back to watching the show. Even then however she couldn't forget the noise in the bushes and began glancing over.

Eventually, after suffering through what seemed like an endless hour of Aussie fractured Christmas, the show finally reached its finale when the Black Ass Chorus began to sing *Here Comes Santa Claus,* but by now they were really feeling their oats because the secret funglu women, wanting to do something special for their very special guest, had added a little something to their coconut funglu drinks and the drinks suddenly kicked in like a fifth or sixth bottle of Three Horses Beer. So now the Black Ass Chorus's version of Here Comes Santa Claus went like,

> *Here comes Santa Claus right down Santa Claus Lane. Dashing, daring, drinking, swearing, lookin' for a poker game.*

As the Black Ass boys crooned their tune, out on the stage came the venerable Popo YoYo sitting atop his sled saying "Ho Ho Ho Popo YoYo." He was dressed from top to bottom with palm fronds that had somehow been painted red. On his head was a tall hat of the same color. His sled however was not being pulled, instead it was being carried by six of the Black Ass boys pretending to be kangaroos and Chow Chow in the lead as MacDugal's fractured Christmas dingo, Roger.

The islanders were delighted because their own Popo YoYo had been crowned as Santa Claus even though they had no clue as to who Santa Claus was and they all stood and applauded and started jumping up and down and singing *dashing, daring, drinking, swearing…*

In the bushes the Chinese, seeing all those beautiful island girls dancing and jumping up and down, began to applaud as well and right there as they thought they weren't being heard, stood the Official Fantasy High Priestess who pointed into the brush and said loudly, "SAMMYTU! SAMMYTU!" because the little Priestess thought their new visitors were just like their other new visitors and would speak English like Sammytu. The little Priestess continued to yell, "SAMMYTU! SAMMYTU!" until everyone in the village paused, grew silent, and looked to see what she was yelling about.

Then the actual Sammytu walked slowly to the bushes, spread them apart and peaked in to discover the Chinese mercenaries sitting frozen, unable to take their eyes off of Sammytu's well formed tits. "Hi," said Sammytu in her father's version of English, "How the fuck are ya? Me Sammytu. You want goddamn funglu?"

Chapter 27

HALO Folks, Just Dropping In

As Sammytu stood and stared at the Chinese mercenaries and the Chinese mercenaries stood and stared back at Sammytu's incredible tits, the rest of the islanders, all wearing only welcoming smiles, walked slowly over and surrounded them. The Chinese didn't seem to pay much attention to the collection of Americans standing nearby because they were now too busy gawking at all the lovely naked women, especially the taller hot Anglo women standing in the midst of the group. And of course smiles always generate more smiles, especially when that smile is on a body that looks like it just came out of a Playboy magazine.

The Black Ass boys were wondering - because they suddenly remembered why they were there in the first place - if they should sprint for their weapons or what? Not that it mattered because they didn't even know where their weapons and gear or even their clothes were anyway. Not to mention the fact they were all pretty well juiced on the holiday funglu cocktail. After a brief discussion they finally concluded their only option was to join the islanders and welcome the new strangers who were already being peacefully relieved of their weapons and gear... and clothes... and of course, were being plied with the holiday funglu cocktail.

It didn't take long for the Black Ass boys to realize there was no threat by their recently discovered arrivals and they soon went back to their Christmas reveling with dancing and song.

Here comes Santa Claus, here comes Santa Claus right down Santa Claus lane.

Dashing, daring, drinking, swearing, lookin' for a poker game.

Everyone will have some fun when good ol' Santa gets laid.

Cause when he's done before the sun the girls will all get paid.

The Chinese wasted no time joining in the party even though they really had no idea what was going on. What they did know was that whatever was happening was a lot more fun and far less dangerous than what they thought they would be doing here for Chun-mei Fu Quang. And if they were going to be put in Chun-mei Fu Quang's annual *bye bye 500 death club* then what better way to go. Some of them even tried to join in the songs of the Black Ass boys even though they had no idea what they were singing. That is except for the multi-lingual Lee Wang and Lee Wang didn't seem to give a shit.

"Hey, Corky," said Herpie, "These guys look a lot like NVA. I'm thinkin' maybe we should shoot 'em. What you think?"

"I'm thinking you got your brains in your ass," said Corky. "That war is over. We lost, remember?"

"Yeah, but that doesn't mean we have to like it."

"It means we don't have a say either way, dumb ass. We walked out, our whole country walked out. That's how they won," said T-Bone. "So how come you want to start shootin' NVA all of a sudden?"

"No special reason. Just one of those days when I feel like shootin' somebody. You know, like maybe somebody who told me I had herpes when I actually didn't."

"Oh, you found out about that, huh?" said T-Bone.

"Yeah, and I think I'm gonna kill Crazy Bob cause it was all his idea."

"Why kill Crazy Bob? It was just a joke?"

"A forty year long joke," said Herpie.

"Okay, but wait until after Christmas," said T-Bone.

"Yeah, okay."

"And don't shoot any of those guys over there because they're not NVA, they're Chinese," said Corky.

"Well isn't that the same thing?" asked Herpie.

"Yeah, but not if you're Chinese," said T-Bone.

"I think I'm gonna get some more of that funglu stuff cause I'm ready to ride," said Herpie as he walked away.

"You really think he's gonna shoot Crazy Bob?" asked T-Bone.

"Nah," said Corky. "He can't see well enough to shoot straight anymore anyway."

"Good. Let's go join the party," said T-Bone.

"Good idea," said Corky. And they walked into the crowd in the center of the village where Popo YoYo was still parading around in his red palm fronds Santa costume saying, "Ho Ho Ho Popo YoYo Ho Ho Ho!"

30,000 feet above the island an aircraft circled while the Delta team completed the final check of their gear and jump rigs.

"Hey, Ambassador," said Nino Bambino. "If this is just a little island with a bunch of horny pigs or even an international collection of killers, why the hell are we doing a HALO drop? Why not go quick and low, or maybe even on the water?"

"Shut the fuck up, Sergeant Bambino," said the Ambassador.

"Uh, Okay, sure," said Bambino.

"Good question," said Robert E. leaning toward the Ambassador. He said it softly to avoid the hard bitten response that Fulgenzi had given his other team member. "We're all thinking the same thing. Why take the risk? I'd like an answer, Ambassador, because everything about this job is a little hinky."

"Hinky?" said Ambassador Fulgenzi.

Captain Robert E. nodded his head, "Hinky."

Just then the aircraft commander came back to address the Ambassador. "Ma'am. We got one seriously bad storm rolling in which gives us only about 15 more minutes in this orbit. Any more than that and I'm turning this aircraft around and heading home to the Lincoln. What's it going to be?"

The ambassador looked at the pilot for a moment, made her decision and turned to Captain Robert E., "Rack 'em and stack 'em, Captain. Let's get this team the hell off this bird."

Captain Robert E. signaled his Delta team. They all put on their oxygen masks then began to move to the back of the aircraft as the big door slowly lowered and in rolled the cold air common to the 30,000 foot altitude.

"You sure you don't want to jump tandem there Ambassador?" asked Sgt. Forester sarcastically.

"Remind me to kick your ass later, Sergeant," said Ambassador Stella Fulgenzi as she jumped from the tail of the plane.

This woman is a strange bird. I wonder where they grow women like that, thought Captain Robert E. as he waddled, heavily loaded with gear, to the rear opening beside his final jumper who happened to be Sgt. Bambino.

"Don't know about you, Captain, but I got a feeling this crazy bitch is jumping us into a real weird shindig. Sure hate to die on Christmas."

"Shut the fuck up, Bambino," came the Ambassador's shrill voice through Bambino's headset.

Captain Robert E. laughed and pointed to the headset in his helmet to remind Bambino that they were all tied together via radio which means the Ambassador heard his every word. He then gave a thumbs up to Bambino and they both fell forward out of the aircraft.

As they flew through the night sky each member focused on the dim blinking light attached to the back of Ambassador Fulgenzi's parachute pack which brought them closer together in their free fall. The parachutes were set to automatically deploy at 1500 feet if the jumper failed to deploy on his or her own which arrived in only minutes. The parachutes opened in succession and they all paraded quietly through the sky over the island. Below they could make out the white sands of part of the island's coastline and beach and a little further inland among the tall palm trees they saw a number of small flickering lights. Falling closer they could now see the larger light created by the main fire in the center of the village.

"Damn!" said Sergeant Bambaino. "There's a bunch of people down there. Don't look like horny pi... OH SHIIIT!" yelled Bambino. He had just lost his main parachute when a whirling gust of wind twisted it into a pretzel. The parachutes of the others were caught up in the wind as well but were still intact and they were scattered in various directions from the village.

Nino Bambino was in a momentary panic until he cut away his main parachute and pulled his reserve. The reserve seemed to take forever to deploy and when it finally did, Bambino looked down just as he crashed through the fronds of a tall coconut palm. His parachute caught in the tree top and jerked him back as he fell toward the ground. Relieved he had survived, he looked to the top of the tree to see how securely his reserve parachute had caught and then he looked down to find out just how far he was from the ground before he would cut himself free. When he looked down he suddenly found he was looking at a startled crowd of buck ass naked people of various races all staring back at him.

"What the fuck?" exclaimed Bambino.

"SAMMYTU! SAMMYTU! SAMMYTU!" pointed the little Priestess. "SAMMYTU!"

Chapter 28

妈的！

"妈的！ **美国人正在入侵！**" yelled one of the Chinese mercenaries, meaning, "Oh shit! The Americans are invading!"

"What did he say," asked Crazy Bob.

"He said, Oh shit! Americans!" replied Lee Wang.

"We're Americans. How come he didn't yell 'Oh shit!' when he saw us?"

"Because you're naked and don't have guns," replied Lee Wang. "He just thought you were crazy."

"Hey, how come you speak perfect English?"

"Because I was born in San Francisco."

"So what are you doing with these Chinese dudes?" asked Corky.

"Didn't like San Fran anymore. Too many gays and Mexicans and freeloaders, also a warrant on me for stealing hot cars. Lots of hot cars," said Lee Wang.

"Oh, that's cool," said Crazy Bob.

"Americans? Americans?" said T-Bone. "Hey you up there. Are you American?"

Bambino looked down, hesitated, then said, "Born and bred *Italian* American… and part Irish, and proud of it. Just want you to know that before you kill me."

"He thinks we're going to kill him," T-Bone said softly to Corky before he looked back up to Bambino, "Tell you what, if you got any Raliegh cigarettes on ya we'll spare your life… or maybe a Snickers bar."

"Good move," said Lee Wang to T-Bone. "You got to take advantage of every opportunity and always get what you can when you can, as my old grandpa used to say."

"Smart ol' man," said T-Bone. "He still at it in San Fran?"

"Nah," said Lee Wang. "He got shot trying to hustle a Black Panther with some phony opium. The guy shot him dead then went and blew up a cop station."

"Oh, too bad. Sorry."

"That's okay. He had a nice long life. About 98 years old I think. Not sure because he quit counting somewhere in his eighties."

"The Black Panther?"

"No, my grandfather."

"Oh, cool," said T-Bone.

"Hey man, I ain't got no Snickers bars and nobody smokes anymore," said Bambino. "So how 'bout you get me down from here and we talk this thing over?

Hate to get killed on Christmas just because I don't smoke."

"Nobody smokes anymore? When did that happen?" asked T-Bone.

"Oh, you know. It was those Clinton people in the White House. They sued all the tobacco companies and won and then the price of cigarettes quadrupled and the next thing you know everybody started to quit because they cost too much. And then you couldn't smoke in restaurants or public buildings or even in your own apartment. Can you imagine that? They're even trying to stop people from smoking in their own car. Hell, they don't even put ashtrays and lighters in the damn things anymore. I tell ya, the worlds going to shit. Hell, man, somehow that even raised the price of pot which was weird because all those Clinton people smoke it. Don't make no sense. Anyhow, I don't have any smokes."

"Yeah, know whatcha mean," said T-Bone. "I remember once when…"

"Shut the fuck up, Bambino!" came the Ambassador's voice from behind the crowd. "And get out of that damn tree."

They all turned to discover Ambassador Fulgenzi standing fast with her M-4 at the ready. At her side stood the rest of the Delta team who had begun to lower their weapons and simply gawk at the group of naked people.

"I claim this island on behalf of the United States of America and as such it is now our protectorate," said the Ambassador. "And if anybody doesn't like it we will blow their asses off the planet. Got that?"

"No, we *don't got that*," came a voice from the village crowd. "This is our island and you can get the hell off."

Out of the group strolled Slammin' Sammy Sinclair in all of her nude glory who walked up face to face with Ambassador Stella Fulgenzi. They stared each other down for the longest minute until the Ambassador lowered her weapon and they embraced and kissed – a long wet kiss.

"Okay Captain, I'm startin' to get a little confused," said Sgt. Forester.

"What can I say," said Captain Robert E., "You know… Washington. There's no accounting for what they call diplomacy now days."

Up in the coconut tree hung Sergeant Bambino who watched in disbelief. Then while everyone stood and watched Slammin' Sammy and Stella swap spit, he pulled his knife, cut his lines and fell to the ground.

"SAMMYTU," said the little Priestess.

"HO HO HO Popo YoYo!" said Popo YoYo.

"You guys don't work for the FBI do you?" asked Herpie.

"Here come Santa dashin' darin'," said the villagers as they dismissed the entire scene and started dancing.

Chapter 29

Captain Who?

"I duh Captain now," said the boss Somali pirate to Tex the Big Bopper. "And where's your good shitter?"

"You know there partner that it jus' ain't good etiquette to come in a man's house and tell him that your takin' it from him and then ask for the shitter," said Tex. "No sirreeee, ain't right at all."

"What house? I no see no house. What you talkin' about white guy?"

Just then young Tarabi leaned over the side of the Yellow Rose and started to barf again.

"What the hell's wrong with that boy," asked Big Little Yankee Dude.

"He pukin," said the pirate boss.

"Yeah, I kinda got that, but why is he pukin'," asked Big Little Yankee Dude.

"Cause he da pump man," said the pirate boss.

"Yeah, so why is he pukin?" said BL.

"Cause he been pumpin," said the boss pirate. "Because he da pump man."

"Yeah, okay, so *he da pump man*," mocked BL. "But he don't look like *no man*. Looks more like a little boy, you ask me."

"He da new guy. Dat why he da pump man," said the boss pirate. "Don't you know nothin'?"

"Yeah, okay," said BL as he shrugged his shoulders and looked to Tex. "I'm thinkin' all these good ol' boys ain't all there in the noggin, Tex. And I'm thinkin' maybe they done out-welcomed their welcome, you ask me."

"Yeah, reckon you're right there, BL. Reckon you're about right on that one."

"Well, sir," said Tex to the boss pirate, "it's time for you to meet my friends, Mr. Smith and Mr. Wesson."

"And Miss Winchester," added Big Little Yankee Dude.

"Who dat people?" asked the boss Somali pirate.

"Let me introduce you," said Tex.

"Good. Dat a good ting cause I da Captain now."

"Yep, you sure are," said Tex, who with lightning speed pulled out his preferred Smith & Wesson shooter and put a round dead into the heart of the boss pirate.

Big Little Yankee Dude quickly followed with three rounds from his Lady Winchester into three of the other pirates. And another got popped by Tex.

"Okay folks, time for you to leave," Tex said to the still standing Somali pirates as he wiggled his gun in the direction of their old boat that was still tied to the side of the Yellow Rose. They immediately began hustling over the side and into their sinking ship. The last was Tarabi who just before he headed for the rail was snatched by Tex and held back. "Not you kid," said Tex. "I'm thinkin' that old boat ain't a place for you. I'm thinkin' you might be a bit happier being a cowboy on the Yellow Rose Ranch."

As he spoke, Big Little Yankee Dude was tossing bodies over the side.

The actual captain of the Yellow Rose stood next to Tarabi, wide eyed after watching the entire episode.

"Um… sir, as I was about to inform you prior to, uh… well, there's a hellacious storm coming on us and it's coming on real fast. In fact, it has turned into a fully certified typhoon, a bad one. It's so bad in fact they've even named it MacArthur which I guess is appropriate since he was a big blowhard."

"I tend to agree," said Big Little Yankee Dude.

"Agree about what?" asked Tex.

"MacArthur. Namin' a hard blowin' typhoon after a blowhard general like MacArthur," replied BL.

"We need to put into some kind of harbor and find shelter or we're going to end up in the drink with those pirate guys," said the Captain.

"Well whatcha think we oughta do, Captain?" asked Tex.

"Well, sir, there's only one thing we can do. That island we're heading for has a lagoon that according to the satellite photos is deep enough and big enough to hold the Yellow Rose. We might have just enough time to reach it and tie up before MacArthur hits us. I'm afraid that's the best we can do. In fact, that's all we can do."

"Well then, kick this here horse in the ass and get us there pretty damn quick, Captain. I sure don't wanna be floppin' around in a dark ocean durin' a storm with a buncha dead Somalis. Sides, bein' a Texas born boy, I ain't much for the aquatics thing," said Tex. "No sirreee, not much for that shit at all. How 'bout you, BL?"

"Hell, Tex, I'm too old for that swimmin' around crap. You know that. Never did like it much, especially after I got my ass bit by some underwater critter down there in Baja. Sides, don't want my lady here to get lost in the deep blue drink. Bad binness you ask me."

"Oh, Captain," said Tex, "you can tell the cook there ain't gonna be no guest for supper. Oh, and do somethin' with this little skinny barf fella here would ya. You know, like maybe a shower and some new cloths and shit."

"Yes sir," said the captain as he turned away. He quickly made his way to the bridge all the while thinking how he should have taken the job on that gambling ship out of New Orleans where he wouldn't have had to put up with all this crazy shit by some low IQ rich rednecks but instead mostly just low IQ rich widows who only wanted to play the slots. "Yes sir," he mumbled to himself. "Whatever you say, sir. Would you like me to kiss your ass, sir? Would you like me to clean your pistol so I can blow your head off, sir? I hope we sink and you drown… sir."

"Oh, and Captain," said Tex. "Have the steward bring us out a couple more a them bottles of Yellow Rose Ranch Texas Rye Whisky will ya? And a couple them chasers," Added Tex. "You wantin' some chasers with your rye there BL?"

"Oooooh I reckon I could do a few," said BL "How 'bout you there little computer man? Some chasers with your Rye?"

On the deck curled up in the farthest corner sat the millennial techhead Alvin who simply stared wide eyed, still replaying in his mind what he had just seen the two Yellow Rose men do with their preferred weapons. He sat thinking to himself, *I don't need rye whisky and I don't need a chaser, I need... I need.... Oh shit, beam me up Scotty – PLEASE!*

Chapter 30

Because Mahmoud Says So

"But I've never read this in the Holy Quran. Tell me where I can read this in the Holy Quran and tell me why we are going to invade this small island so far away," said the young soldier member of the 12 man team of Iranian Revolutionary Guard.

"You have many questions, my young soldier. Is it not enough for you to know we are serving Allah?" replied the young soldier's commanding officer. "It is Mohamed's wish we do this thing."

"But I don't think Mohamed ever flew halfway around the world to conquer an island full of fornicating pigs. Not even if they are infidel pigs, which, of course, are all pigs."

"These pigs are the guardians of great wealth and power and we have been chosen," said his commander.

"Chosen by whom, and for what? I am not so sure it was Mohamed or even Allah," said the young soldier,

"And why are these infidel pigs so different that Mohamed would choose us to destroy them. They are so far away and no threat to Islam. I'm inclined to utilize an old and wise American bit of wisdom that states, *If it ain't broke, don't fix it.*"

"American! Tell me where you came by those American words of heresy? Have you been reading the literature of those infidels instead of the Holy Quran?"

"No sir," said the young soldier. "I heard it on the radio. It was spoken or quoted in song by the late great Johnny Cash. Do you know he once fell into a ring of fire and returned to sing about it?"

"You must not believe anything you hear from the Americans. They are all infidels of mixed blood and they cohabit with Jews. With Jews! Is that what you want? To fill your head with bad wisdom from Jews and infidels, people who eat their own children and bacon? You must ask forgiveness from Mohamed and pray to Allah."

"But..."

"No boy! There is no excuse. This Johnny Cash man is evil and all that he says is evil. He is American and he will be wiped off the face of the earth like all American infidels."

"But... sir, he is already dead."

"There, you see. Mohamed has struck him down and now it is our place in this anti-pig caliphate to do the same."

"But... pigs?" said the young soldier.

"Commander," called the pilot from the cockpit of the American made C-130.

"You must pray for forgiveness," the Iranian Revolutionary Colonel told the young soldier as he rose and went to the cockpit. "Yes, what is it?"

"We have entered a storm that seems to be heading in the same direction as we and it has also somehow come in behind us."

"Come in behind us? You mean you foolish shits flew right into it. I thought you people were supposed to know how to avoid these things," complained the Iranian Colonel.

"Yes sir, we do, but first we have to know where it is and this is an American plane that we bought from ISIS and we can't read all those controls for the radar and radio that tell us the weather and if there is a storm. Therefore, we have now been trapped into a storm."

"You idiot! Where were you taught to fly?" yelled the Colonel.

"Uh… in Russia, sir. But they didn't read English either. And if they did, they sure didn't let us know about it. Probably because they were always consuming great quantities of vodka. Infidels, all infidels."

"So now what are we going to do?" asked the Colonel.

"Well, sir, there's an old wise saying that goes; *Keep your face away when the shit hits the fan.*"

"And where did you come by that wisdom?" asked the Colonel.

"I saw it on TV, sir. On the Comedy Channel."

"Shit," said the colonel. "We're all going to die."

"By the way, sir," said the pilot, "would you be so kind as to tell us why we are on this mission?"

"Because Mahmoud Ahmadinejad said so," replied the Colonel.

"But he's not the President anymore," said the pilot.

"Don't believe everything you hear," said the colonel. "Mahmoud speaks directly for Mohamed to all Muslims and he is our Commander and Chief," said the colonel as he returned to the rear of the plane.

"And he is an asshole," mumbled the pilot. "Damn, we're all going to die," he exhaled as he began to play with the various switches in the cockpit.

"What are you doing?" asked the co-pilot.

"I'm trying to find the radar thing so we can figure out how to get out of this storm," said the pilot.

"Shit," said the co-pilot. "We're all going to die." Just then the plane jerked and banked and the co-pilot looked out the window and saw one of the starboard engines was on fire. القرف المقدس! ما الذي فعلته؟ said the co-pilot, meaning; "Holy shit! What did you do?"

"What do you mean, what did I do? All I did was flip some switches.

"But you set the engine on fire."

"No, all I did was flip this switch like this," said the pilot as he flipped the switch. The aircraft suddenly bucked and jolted and when he looked out the window he saw one of the port engines had burst into flames.

القرف المقدس! لقد فعلتها مجددا. yelled the co-pilot, meaning, "Holly shit! You did it again!"

The pilot began flipping switches all over the cockpit and finally the engine fires went out but the engines did not start back up.

"You got to get those engines back on. We can't fly through this storm with only two engines," said the co-pilot.

"Oh, alright," said the pilot. And he began flipping more switches. Then suddenly both the port and starboard engines that were still running quit.

"Now what did you do?" asked the co-pilot.

"I didn't do anything. I just flipped some switches."

"Well, quit flipping switches or we are all going to die," said the co-pilot.

The Pilot quit flipping switches but the engines didn't come back on and the plane began to rapidly lose altitude when all of a sudden all four engines burst into flames.

"What is going on? Why are we losing altitude? What are we doing?" said the colonel of the Iranian Revolutionary Guard.

"We are all going to die," said the co-pilot.

"We are not going to die. Mahmoud Ahmadinejad will not permit it," said the Colonel.

"Fuck Mahmoud Ahmadinejad," said the pilot. "Mahmoud Ahmadinejad is not flying this plane."

"Apparently neither are you," said the angry Revolutionary Guard colonel as he pulled out his pistol and shot the pilot in the head. He then turned to the co-pilot, pointed the pistol and said, "Now, who is flying this plane?"

"Well, it sure as hell isn't him," said the co-pilot. "And you might as well shoot me too because in one minute we are all going to meet Allah."

"Then why don't you fly the plane?" asked the colonel.

"Because the engines have quit running."

"Why have the engines quit running," asked the colonel.

"I'm not sure but I think it might have something to do with the fact they are on fire and you shot the pilot," said the co-pilot.

"Then fly the plane. Aren't you a pilot?"

"No I'm not a pilot. I'm the pilot's brother-in-law. I'm just here because we were going to stop off in Singapore and get laid on the way home." The co-pilot looked out the cockpit window and saw the ocean coming at them full speed and started to mumble a Catholic prayer.

"What are you doing?" demanded the colonel.

"I'm praying because we are all going to die," said the co-pilot.

"That is not a Muslim prayer," yelled the colonel. "That is an infidel's prayer."

"Yes, well, we all have our little secrets don't we," said the co-pilot who then resumed his Catholic prayer, "Our father who art it heaven…"

BANG!

Chapter 31

 Bucks & Booz

"Lookin' pretty nasty out there, Tex. Yep, seems that storm is rollin' in pretty nasty," said Big Little Yankee Dude as he sipped his Texas Yellow Rose Rye Whiskey.

"Yep," said Tex.

"You see how that ol' Somali boat went down out there? Jus' kina listed and lobbed around thar till it flipped over. And all them skinny pirates fellas standin' on that upside down boat wavin' there arms around and shit. It was kina poetic, you ask me."

"Yep," said Tex. "Kina poetic."

"Water's gettin' kina rough here, Tex."

"Yep," said Tex.

"Reckon we gonna make it to that island?"

"Yep," said Tex.

"What makes you so sure?" asked BL.

"Cause if we don't and we die out here, then I'm gonna fire that damn captain," said Tex.

"Yep, that's my ol' Tex. Don't tolerate no failure in the Texas Yellow Rose Corporation. I think your daddy'd be mighty proud."

"Yep," said Tex.

"Hey, looky there in the sky," said Big Little Yankee Dude. "Think that's some kina shootin' star or sompin'?"

"Nope. Looks like one of them Army planes gets shot down in the movies. Looky there, I think it's on fire alright," said Tex.

"Yep," said Big Little Yankee Dude.

"Yep," agreed Tex.

"This sure has been one hell of a interestin' boat ride, you ask me."

"Yep."

"Hey, Tex. What say I bet you a hunerd thousand bucks that that thar plane hits that thar upside down pirate boat when it crashes?"

"Yep, I'll take that bet and I'll throw in a full case of rye whisky to boot."

"Done deal."

The two men sat on the deck of the rolling yacht and watched with interest as the plane came down in flames and crashed into the ocean with a fiery burst.

"Whatcha think there, BL? Think it hit the target?"

"Tell ya in a minute when all the smoke and fire and shit clears. Yep, yep, here we go. Startin' to clear up a bit now. Heeeere we gooooo. HEEEE HAAAWWW!" said Big Little Yankee Dude. "It looks like you be owin' ol' BL here some bucks and booz thar ol' Tex."

"Yep," said Tex.

Out in the ocean, just beyond the wreck and collision of the Iranian aircraft and Somali pirate boat, the young Revolutionary Guard Soldier pulled himself up on a piece of flotsam. As he wiped the water from his face he looked into the far distance and saw the silhouette of a small island. *Okay*, he thought to himself, *if Johnny Cash can fall into a burning ring of fire and survive, then he, Forood son of Siavosh Parviz, can surely defeat the sea.*

Chapter 32

Disco Dino

It had been an hour since the Delta team had landed on the island, during which time they had been disarmed, undressed, and loaded with *Christmas Holiday Funglunog*. Everyone on the island was feeling exceptionally randy and looking forward to a long night of group sex, especially the newcomer Chinese and Deltas who were also surprised as hell to discover that their feared leader was the former girlfriend of Slammin' Sammy Sinclair which of course explained her undying desire to take the island. The Ambassador had all the intel and the intel told her that Slammin' Sammy was already there so she easily convinced the President to give her the mission. She had been searching for Slammin' Sammy for six years, ever since they had a brief affair in London during a G20 Summit where Slammin' Sammy was protesting the Pepsi Cola company for supporting Progressive politicians. Finding and just keeping up with

Slammin' Sammy was a difficult task, even when you have all the resources of the U.S. Government at your service. She had a tendency to jump from cause to cause to either protest or support those causes, and in between there were short stints in various jails around the world after she would kick someone's ass. All the while Ambassador Stella Fulgenzi pined for that incredible woman she met it London and she had finally found her on Whatchamacalit Island.

Captain Robert E. watched as two of the most beautiful women he had ever seen in his entire life's existence poured over each other during the festivities and he nearly cried with disappointment knowing he had no chance in hell of hooking up with either one. Just the same he did look forward to a pleasant stay with *a* or *many* of the lovely native girls, all the while keeping in mind that whatever happened on this particular island was far better than looking for the President's retarded dog, Consti.

Captain Robert E. kicked back against a hut and watched as the Delta boys, danced with the native girls and the Chinese mercenaries danced with the native girls and the Black Ass boys danced with the native girls and sometimes the Delta boys danced with the Chinese boys who sometimes danced with the Black Ass guys and everyone simply had a ball. Meanwhile, the little Priestess danced and laughed alone yelling, "SAMMYTU, SAMMYTU!"

Just as Captain Robert E. was about to consume his third cup of holiday funglunog he noticed all the crowd had formed a circle and were clapping in rhythm while someone stood in the center singing. He rose and strolled over to find in the center of the crowd was Sergeant Nino Bambino dancing and going disco with Sammytu and singing with the melody from Copacabana saying;

> *My name is Nino, Nino Bambino,*
> *And everywhere I go I want everyone to know,*
> *I am Nino, Nino Bambino,*
> *Love all the ladies and drive them all crazy,*
> *Because with Niiiiiinooo, they fallllll in looooove,*
> *Nino Bambiiiiiinoooooo*

Dancing around Nino and Sammytu was the little Priestess singing, "Sammytu, Sammytu, Saaaaaamytuuuuu." Watching this scene Captain Robert E. wondered if indeed there ever was a Delta soldier somewhere inside Nino's body, especially since his only combat experience was finding a retarded dog.

The thoughts of Captain Robert E. were interrupted when he was approached by Corky. "Pretty tough assignment, wouldn't you say?" asked Corky.

Captain Robert E. laughed, "An understatement."

"Yeah, these folks have a way of lifting your soul don't they?"

"Sure do."

"Be ashamed to ruin them with a bunch of greed and misguided values from the so-called civilized world."

"Sure would," agreed Captain Robert E.

"Just wondering, who sent you boys here anyway?" asked Corky.

"Oh, nobody special. Just the President," said Captain Robert E. "How 'bout you?"

"Some uber rich Texan. A total shitstick you ask me."

"Yeah, they usually are."

Just then they were joined by Lee Wang. "I'd have to agree with you there."

"So who sent you here?" asked Corky.

"Some dickhead who wants to rule China. And get rich while doing it," said Lee Wang.

"You got to wonder why they want this place so bad. Too far away from the rest of the world to be a resort. Can't see it means anything to anybody except these nice islanders."

"You mean you don't know?" said Lee Wang.

"Know what," asked Captain Robert E.

"This island. It's loaded with gold and diamonds and oil and get this… uranium to."

"Are you sure?" asked Corky. "That Texan told us he was looking for the bones of Amelia Earhart. Said she was his grandmother."

"Nah. That's a load of crap. I got it straight from the little Russian guy who was sent here by Vladimir Putin."

"What Russian guy?" asked Captain Robert E.

"The one I got tied to a tree back there by the lagoon."

"You got a Russian tied to a tree?"

"Sure. We were going to kill him but he started spilling the beans so we let him live. What the hell, no skin off my nose."

"SAMMYTU! SAMMYTU! SAMMYTU!"

All three men looked to the circle where the little Priestess, Nino, and Sammytu were all dancing and laughing hand and hand.

Corky wondered what they were dancing to since there was no music or drums but figured that with the holiday funglunog nobody needed music anyway.

"So, you got a Russian," said Captain Robert E.

"Yeah."

"He dangerous?" asked Corky.

"Nah. He's just some goofy nerd type. Can't stay out of his own way. You know the type," said Lee Wang.

"Yeah," said Robert E. and Corky in unison.

"Gold, diamonds, oil, uranium? Can't say anybody would need that shit in a place like this," said Corky.

"You got a point there," agreed Lee Wang.

"Can't say I'm in a big hurry to get back. Nothing there but a bitchy wife. The rest of my team are single. So are you guys thinking what I'm thinking?" said Captain Robert E.

"Don't think my boys will complain," said Corky.

"We can't go back," said Lee Wang. "We go back and Chun-mei Fu Quang will execute us all because we didn't get him his prize."

"Whoa, bummer," said Corky. "So the task is how to stay and keep the rest of the world away."

"I think I can take care of that," came a voice from behind.

They turned to find Ambassador Stella Fulgenzi looking real fine.

"And just how would you do that?" asked Corky.

"Oh, just by using a little diplomatic ass kicking," she smiled.

Chapter 33

MacArthur Blows!

Thirty minutes ago the Yellow Rose had become caught up in the storm and was rolling and pitching like a wild bronco. Both Tex and Big Little Yankee Dude, along with the millennial techhead Alvin, the pirate pump man Tarabi, and half the crew, were all hanging it over the side barfing. The boat captain had just joined them for a quick puke himself before he would return to the bridge.

"What the hell you doin' here, Cap'n? Ain't you spose ta be driving the boat?" yelled Tex.

"The first mate is… blaaauugh… at the wheel right now sir," replied the captain.

"Well, what the fuck, man. Why ain't we… blaaaauugf… at that island already?" said Tex.

The captain tried to speak but was fighting back another upchuck so he just pointed out across the water.

When Tex followed his finger he saw the island a short distance away.

"Maybe fifteen or twenty minutes... BLAAAUUUG UHG, yuk... and we'll be there," said the captain. "...having to fight the sea. But we'll make..." Blaaauuug. "We'll make it."

"This is a big... blaaaaug... boat here Cap'n. How come it's ridin' so damn wild?" asked Big Little Yankee Dude. "I thought this damn thing's got stabilizers and shit."

"Well, it's... a... bluuuuaaaaagh... a big ass storm, sir," said the captain. "And stabilizers... blaaaugh... stabilizers can only do so much."

"Ain't nothin' can't be tamed, Cap'n," said Tex. "Now get your ass... blaaaauug... up yonder on that bridge and get us to that fuckin' island pretty damn quick afore we end up in the water with them skinny pirate boys."

The Captain was too nauseous to speak so he simply nodded and went to the bridge.

"I'm thinkin' this here's the worse fuckin' thing I ever done," said Big Little Yankee Dude. "Kinda makes ya... blaauuugh... makes ya... blaaaaaaaugh... makes ya wish ya was never born, you ask me."

"Yep. Blaaaaaauuugh."

In the midst of the Christmas festival the dancing Santa Claus, Popo YoYo, froze and stood tall. He looked out to the sea then into the trees and the sky and immediately began to yell a bunch of stuff that none or

the newly arrived foreigners understood until he pointed
desperately to the open sea. Suddenly all the islanders
began to scurry in all directions about the village
collecting their small children and most of their valuable
belongings. Those who didn't have children took the
Anglos and the Chinese by the arm and began leading
them toward the lagoon.

"Sammytu," called Slammin' Sammy. "What's
happening?"

"Bad sky!" said Sammytu. "Bad time sky. Bad wind.
Make big fuckin' mess! Come with me fast," she said as
she took both Slammin' Sammy and Nino by the arm and
pulled them along with the others.

Ambassador Stella looked to the sky and immediately
knew what Sammytu was saying. It was a massive storm,
a typhoon. "My god," she said to herself. "Where will
these people go for safety?" She quickly decided that the
island people were the only ones who knew what to do in
a severe storm on a small island in the Pacific and she
followed the crowd.

As they all fled for safety Corky assisted an elderly
woman by carrying her things and Captain Robert E.
snatched up the little Priestess and tossed her on his back.
"SAMMYTU!" she cried out with a broad smile.
"SAMMYTU!"

All the people on the island scurried along a narrow
trail through some dense jungle until they arrived at the
lagoon where the Black Ass boys had come in on their
zodiac. Popo YoYo led the pack as they rounded the

lagoon and began climbing up a stone hill for about thirty feet where they reached a large opening into a deep cavernous tunnel. Stored against the wall was an assortment of torches and flints that were lit by islanders as they entered and paraded further into the darkness with their children and their goods. When the Black Ass boys reached the back of the cave they were amazed to find it was already equipped with everything they would need to survive the time it would take to avoid the dangers of a storm. And even more surprising was along the back side of the large cave, neatly placed and stacked, was their gear and weapons.

"I'll be a son of a bitch," said Sergeant Forester with a smile. "I thought they probably tossed this shit into the sea."

"Maybe they should have," said T-Bone.

"Yeah, you might be right there, bro," said Nino.

When all the people of the island settled in, Popo YoYo with assistance from Slammin' Sammy took a count and decided everyone was accounted for. Outside could be heard the winds as they slammed across the island and began bending the trees and tearing apart the huts in the village, but to the surprise of all the new arrivals, the islanders showed no fear or sense of loss to their homes.

"What wonderful people," said Ambassador Fulgenzi.

"Yes," agreed Slammin' Sammy. "They accept what they can't change without concern. We have to protect them."

"I just have one question," said the Ambassador.

"What's that?" said Slammin' Sammy.

"Is it true they eat their dead?"

"Wellllll, yeah, kind of," said Slammin' Sammy.

"Kind of? What's that mean?"

"Well, they only eat the good ones. It's a form of love, honor, and respect. The others they throw in the ocean. You would really have to be a complete and totally hated asshole before they would even think of not eating you and tossing you into the ocean. So, it's a love hate sort of thing. And they don't kill anybody. They wait until they die naturally. But what the hell. It's a tradition and traditions are a good thing. Don't you think?"

"Um... guess so," said the Ambassador. "I've seen worse in Washington."

"What can I say; *waste not want not*, right?"

Captain Robert E. sat down next to Lee Wang and struck up a conversation to pass the time. "Sounds pretty nasty out there."

"Sure does," said Lee Wang.

"Hate to be out there in it. Typhoon winds, debris flying everywhere, tidal surge and waves. Can't say anybody could survive that."

"You got that right," said Lee Wang.

"You know I saw this old movie once where these islanders were hit with a typhoon and to keep from getting washed away they tied themselves to trees and..."

"Oh shit!" said Lee Wang.

"Oh shit!" said Captain Robert E. as they both instantly remembered the same thing and both said at the same time, "THE RUSSIAN!"

They both jumped up and looked to each other for an answer to the problem.

"What are we going to do?" asked Captain Robert E.

"Well, uh, we were going to kill him anyway, sooo…"

"Can't do that even if he is a Putin guy," said Captain Robert E. "We don't have any choice. We got to go get him."

"Shit," said Lee Wang. "Oh okay, guess so."

Sammytu had overheard their conversation and put enough English together to figure out what they were going to do and she went directly to Popo YoYo.

As the Captain and Lee Wang headed for the opening of the cave they were intercepted by Popo YoYo who motioned he was going along and told them to follow him. Out they went to discover the storm had arrived in full force over the entire island. When they had come to the village they found most of it had been blown away and the water was coming ever so quickly inland.

"WHERE IS HE," yelled Captain Robert E.

"THERE. OVER THAT WAY," said Lee Wang.

"COME ME. COME ME," yelled Popo YoYo as he dashed off into the wind and into the jungle. They followed and soon arrived at the cluster of coconut trees where the Chinese mercenaries had been hiding. In the middle of the coconut grove was Borris Bolufski still tied to the tree, passed out, and looking like an old wet dish rag.

"Damn, I think he's dead," said Lee Wang.

Captain Robert E. quickly checked the Russian's vitals. "It's okay. He's still alive. We have to get him out of here."

"Shit!" said Lee Wang.

"What's wrong?" said the Captain.

"I don't have a knife. Can't cut him loose."

Captain Robert E. grabbed the rope and started to pull in an effort to break it apart but it was nylon and there was no way he could do it. While still trying he was pushed aside by Popo YoYo who stepped in, took hold of the rope that secured the Russian to the tree and yelled something unintelligible at the top of his voice as he pulled and pulled and pulled until it finally snapped. Borris Bolufski fell to the ground. Captain Robert E. began picking him up when again he was pushed aside by Popo YoYo who snatched and tossed the Russian over his shoulder and took off at a trot.

"That is one strong fuckin' beach boy," said Lee Wang.

"Sure is. Let's go," said Captain Robert E..

They quickly followed Popo YoYo all the way back to the hillside cave. As they were climbing in Captain Robert E. turned and looked out to sea where he thought he caught a glimpse of a big luxury yacht. He wiped the rain from his face and looked again but could only see a short distance through the storm so he turned and entered the safety of the cave. When he arrived at the far end where everyone was gathered he found the village women treating Borris Bolufski by giving him some Christmas Funglunog which was already bringing him to his senses.

Typhoon MacArthur took the better part of the night to pass over the island and in the morning all was bright and sunny, clear and calm. The islanders slowly emerged from the cave and looked out over the lagoon where they found with total amazement, listing to one side and sitting up on dry land, the two hundred forty foot luxury yacht, Yellow Rose.

The Black Ass boys had made their way to the mouth of the cave and, looking out over the lagoon, heard the little Priestess yell, "SAMMYTU! SAMMYTU!" She had made her way to the edge of the lagoon and was standing near a disheveled man who was sitting at the edge of the water with a bottle of Yellow Rose Ranch Texas Rye Whisky. He took a long swig then passed the bottle to another man who was laid out behind him. Both men were soon joined by the crew of the boat, the millennial techhead Alvin, and the pirate pump man Tarabi. They all flopped down on the ground and began passing around the bottle as they stared at the little Priestess as she pointed and yelled, "SAMMYTU! SAMMYTU!"

The man took back the bottle, took a big swig, looked to the boat and said, "Cap'n, I think it's time we renegotiate your fuckin' contract."

"Oh shit," said MacDugal. "Is that the Texas asshole?"

"Yep," said Crazy Bob.

"Did he bring that pizza guy?" asked Herpie. "I hope to hell he brought that pizza guy."

Chapter 34

The Art of the Deal

"I ain't payin' you fellas for fuckin' around here like you's on a vacation. Prob'ly playin' limbo on the beach and shit," said a very angry Tex the Big Bopper as he addressed the Black Ass boys.

"You haven't paid us at all... yet," said MacDugal.

"I'm gonna shoot that damn Aussie," said Tex. "Shut the hell up and listen. I come here cause I thought you boys was in trouble and bein' tortured and shit. And after I get here I find..." He paused and for the first time he realized what he was looking at. "Where the fuck are all yer clothes? How come ain't nobody round here got any clothes on?"

"Ain't sup'n I'd be complainin' about thar, Tex. I mean you see'n that blonde lady over there. She sure as shit ain't sup'n to complain about, you ask me," said Big Little Yankee Dude. "Kina like to get me some that."

"Gotta take care a binness first, BL. Always gotta take care binness before pleasure. Gotta do the deal fore ya spin the wheel. Know what I mean?"

"Sure do, Tex."

"We are fully surrounded by the enemy here so go get yer lady friend."

Big Little Yankee Dude moved off to the boat to retrieve his Winchester.

"Now, where was I?"

"We were talking about how you're not paying us for what we're not doing," said T-Bone.

"What, you some kina smart ass like that damn Aussie boy?"

"I ain't no boy, buster. I'm old enough to be your fa... um, big brother. And I'm thinking I won't have any trouble kicking your long tall Texas ass cause this is one damn Georgia Bulldog you don't wanna mess with."

"Now just a minute. What the hell is going on here and who the hell are you?" said Ambassador Stella Fulgenzi.

"Anybody ever tell you that you're one seriously foxy lady. Long tall and beautiful, you gotta be from Texas darlin'. Now why don't you jus' take a seat someplace while I do the deal here, then we can talk a little, you know... about kinder gentler harmonious types of things."

"I'll be doing the dealing here Mr. Long Tall and Stupid Tex. You got nothing that interests me and if you've got any business regarding this island, you'll do it with me," declared Ambassador Fulgenzi.

"Well darlin' from what I see of you, I can't think of anythin' nicer at the moment, but you see first I got to declare that this here is my island and all you folks are now citizens of the Texas Yellow Rose Corporation who are residin' on the island of Yellow Rose," smiled Tex. "Ain't that a nice name? Named it after my great grandma is what I did. Now with that binness all settled what say you and me go for a stroll on the beach there darlin'."

At that moment Slammin' Sammy walked up and stood next to Stella. Chow Chow came and stood next to Slammin' Sammy. "The name of this island is Wassi... Wassmasio... uh, *Wassimasiomoaki.*" said Slammin' Sammy.

"Yeah, it's Wassmao... uh, Whatchamacallet Island," said Chow Chow.

"What the fuck is that?" said Tex.

"What?" said Stella.

"That little thang there? What the hell is that some kina little people like one of them little Irish munchkin gremlin thangs that dance around and do tricks and mess with people and shit?" laughed Tex. "How 'bout it munchkin, you gonna do us a little magic dance like one a them leppercans?"

"How about'a if I'm'a do a dance on'a your ugly face you tall ignorant *cacca di cane*," said an angry Chow Chow.

"Well looky there, BL. We got us a walkin' talkin' little Italian meatball right here on my island. Hmm...

sorry there little munchkin but short people got no reason for livin' in my world."

"I think you've said enough, Mr. Tall and Stupid. Time for you to leave town," said Stella.

"Leave? Darlin', you and I have just begun to…"

"Honey, is this man bothering you?" Slammin' Sammy asked the Ambassador, interrupting Tex. "Because he sure as hell is bothering me."

"Honey? Well looky there, BL. We got us a twofer goin' on here. Two gorgeous ladies right here on my island. Hot diggity this might turn out to be my day after all."

"Oh don't worry, baby," assured Stella. "It's nothing I can't handle. Isn't that right boys?" she said as she looked to the rear of Tex and Big Little Yankee Dude.

"Absolutely correct, ma'am," said Captain Robert E.

Tex and BL turned to discover the entire Delta team along with the Chinese mercenaries standing buckass naked in full combat gear with their weapons at the ready.

"Well, I'll be damn. Now jus' where the hell'd these here fellas come from," asked Tex with a laugh. "BL, you think that maybe you and me could take care of these here boys?"

"Well, it ain't like we ain't never done it before, Tex. And these here nudie cupcakes should be a piece'a pie like down yonder in Valparaiso, you ask me. Or was that Venezuela?"

"That's a *piece of cake* not a *piece of pie*, you redneck idiot. Hell, even us Australians know that much, mate" said MacDugal.

"That little irritatin' Aussie dude is like a wart on my ass and I'm thinkin' it's time ta cut it off," said Tex as he pulled his Smith & Wesson and shot MacDugal in the shoulder as he ducked to avoid the bullet.

Naturally the Delta boys and the Chinese all responded while everyone else scattered in all directions. Slammin' Sammy, Chow Chow, and Stella grabbed MacDugal and dragged him behind the trees and out of the line of fire where they started treating his wound.

"I AM TEX THE BIG BOPPER AND I DON'T TAKE NO SHIT FROM NOOOOBODY," yelled Tex as he turned to face the Deltas and the Chinese and started shooting. Next to him Big Little Yankee Dude yelling, "Yeeee Hawww!" with his lady Winchester also began shooting.

Two of the Chinese went down and one of the Delta boys hit the ground, all wounded but not critical. Actually the shots fired by Tex and BL were haphazard for no other reason than a three day binge and overdose of Texas Yellow Rose Rye Whiskey while they were passengers on the Yellow Rose yacht. Tex was shooting left when he thought he was shooting right, and Big Little Yankee Dude was shooting down when he thought he was shooting up. The result was Tex was missing and BL was shooting people in the foot.

The response from the Deltas and Chinese was a gruesome thing to see. Let it suffice to say Tex will no longer be practicing the art of the deal... with anybody... ever again, and Big Little Yankee Dude was so loaded with Yellow Rose Rye Whiskey that he actually survived no less than a dozen bullet wounds, healed, assimilated and eventually became a favorite playmate of the island's children... after Nino of course. Both he and Tex were reported lost at sea in Typhoon MacArthur.

Following the mad minute of conflict all returned to normal, except for the storm damage, of course, which took a little time to clean up and repair. All the wounded were cared for, the boat crew helped rebuild the village and the islanders helped to refloat the boat after which Herpie got a steady supply of pizza.

Most all of the new residents including the boat crew elected to start wearing loin clothes simply because they weren't comfortable looking at each others' junk all the time, no matter how much fun it was just flapping in the breeze. Some islanders saw it as a fashion statement and began doing the same thing. Those who chose not to care and didn't wear loin clothes were labeled *exhibitionists* but accepted the label as a point of pride – because, they were exhibitionists – but nobody really cared.

Slammin' Sammy and Stella rekindled their lost London love affair which freed up Chow Chow, who gave up on men to pursue the shortest woman on the island - a direct influence of a steady supply of funglu.

The Delta boys got together and elected to never return to chasing retarded dogs again and to join the Black Ass Deserters Club which was reestablished in a brand new hooch complete with a long bar and a dart board and all the booze from aboard the Yellow Rose. Crazy Bob, who was now a partner with Captain Robert E., estimated the booze should last at least a year and a half and was promised by the boat captain that he would return on a regular basis with a fresh supply of booze and a large supply of Three Horses Beer. The boat captain could make that promise because he and his crew decided they were going to take the Yellow Rose, now renamed *Funglu Freedom*, on a world cruise.

The FBI guys decided to temporarily substitute funglu for Three Horses Beer and in fact improved on the formula. This also allowed them to buy an interest in Popo Yo Yo's action.

MacDugal's wound healed and the scar became a favorite thing for all the island girls to touch and giggle at. No one knows why because the other guys that got wounded did't enjoy the same privilege. Perhaps because they were wounded in the feet.

The millennial techhead, Alvin, inspected all the combat communications gear and decided it didn't offer much of a challenge so he decided to go back to Texas where he hacked the Texas Yellow Rose Corporation's central computer and transferred a very large amount of the company's money to an offshore bank account in the

Caymans. He also set up an account for the boat captain and crew to finance their world travels.

All the invaders eventually settled in and found a niche, built a hut and subsequently found a woman… or two – but still enjoyed funglu and all its group benefits.

The Yellow Rose pizza chef stayed and went to work at the new Black Ass Club as did Tarabi the pump pirate who stayed because he didn't have anywhere else to go.

The Chinese guys turned out to be a great deal of fun, especially when they were working. They all, except Lee Wang, proved to be excellent fishermen, farmers, general all around workers, and serious party animals. Lee Wang continued to hustle them simply because he could.

And finally there was Borris Bolufski. No one was quite sure just what the hell he would do or say if he went back to Russia so the Black Ass and FBI boys convinced him they heard on the radio that Putin had put out a *dead or alive* warrant for his arrest causing him to stay on the island. And they also told him he had herpes.

Ambassador Stella Fulgenzi came up with a diabolical plan to keep the island from further foreign intrusion and to achieve this she hitched a ride on the *Funglu Freedom* yacht back to the States and took Popo YoYo with her.

All things considered, the island became a happy, prosperous, and peaceful place when it returned to being just a lost paradise.

Chapter 35

Six Months Later

Ambassador Stella Fulgenzi walked into the United Nations like she owned the place. Behind her was a barefoot Popo YoYo wrapped in a long silver/white fur coat he had gotten from Joe Namath at a cocktail party the night before by trading a jar of Funglu. The coat had two pockets and what all those people staring at him in the UN didn't know was that in each of those pockets was a handful of large uncut diamonds, the per diem for Stella and Popo YoYo's trip from Whatchamacallet Island to the States and eventually the Big Apple and the United Nations.

The UN assembly was in session but Stella didn't care as she strolled into the center of the large circle of seated so-called dignitaries from around the world with their interpreters babbling into their headsets. They all stared in disbelief. They knew who she was but had never seen or been interrupted with a show and tell that included a strangely dressed native man or any strange man since the visit and incomprehensible speech by Libya's late dictator Muammar Mohammed Abu Minyar Gaddafi who was as daffy as a fruitcake.

"Ambassador Fulgenzi, it has been quite some time since we have seen you and need I tell you that you are out of order and in fact disrupting this assembly," said the Secretary General of the UN, Mr. Ombalega Motoo Wambaga.

"What's the matter Secretary Wambago, afraid the assembly and the rest of the world might find out how you hired a bunch of Somali pirates to invade and claim an island that's not yours so you can exploit its minerals and fossil fuel resources and make a shitpot full of money that would far exceed all the millions you have stolen from UN funds? Don't worry, I won't tell anyone. Oh, by the way, those Somali pirates you hired? They're at the bottom of the sea - all dead now."

The Secretary General paled and sat back trying to avoid the gazes of the collection of the world's representatives as the interpretation of what Stella said came through their individual headsets. After glaring at the little African Secretary General with displeasure when he failed to deny her charges, they all turned their attention to Stella and the strange dark man she had paraded into their midst.

"May I remind you once again you are out of order, Ambassador Fulgenzi," said the Secretary General. "And being you have been replaced by your government, I suggest that you leave this assembly immediately."

"Oh put a sock in it, Wambaga," said Stella. "And don't call me Ambassador because I quit that job."

This particular UN assembly was being broadcast live on FOX News because they were scheduled to vote on something very important that they had nothing to do with but would result in the UN and Wambaga getting more money. Sitting in his office in the White House the President was slithering down some chilled oysters on the half shell for lunch and watching the news. He perked up when he saw Stella enter the fray. "What the fuck," said the President. "Where the hell did she come from? And who's that weird ass polar bear she's got there? And why the hell is he wearing that damn thing in the middle of June?"

"Don't know Mr. President. We thought she was lost with that entire Delta team when they got hit by MacArthur."

"MacArthur? MacArthur? God damn son, haven't you heard? Those wars were over more than half a century ago and MacArthur is dead, deader than a door knob. Don't you know your history? Shit man, I'm thinking it might be time for you to retire."

"I can't retire, Mr. President. I'm the Vice President."

"Don't mean anything. There are lots more fish in the sea, or should I say *the swamp*."

"MacArthur was the name of a typhoon that took place in the Pacific Ocean six months ago where we thought Ambassador Fulgenzi and her team was lost. You know, on that island," said the VP.

"What island?" asked the President.

"You know, that island out there with all that gold and diamonds and oil and uranium that everybody in the world was trying to claim," said the VP. "Remember?"

"Uh... of course I remember. I thought we fixed that crisis."

"Uh, it wasn't a crisis, Mr. President."

"Well then why the hell were we fixing it if it wasn't a crisis?"

"You tell me."

"I'm asking you."

"Don't ask me because I don't know. All I know is we were going to claim it before anybody else could claim it because it has all that good stuff and that uranium."

"So what's Stella, I mean, Ambassador Fulgenzi, doing there at the UN?"

"I'm not sure but we got this message from her through the State Department a few minutes ago."

"Minutes ago? From Stella, I mean the Ambassador? Well hell, what's it say?"

"It says, *I Stella May Fulgenzi do hereby resign my position as the United States Ambassador to the United Nations and give up my citizenship of the United States altogether to become a representative and citizen of the sovereign state of Wassimasiomoaki Island.*"

"What? Wassi what?"

"Uh, Wassi... Wassmio... um, shit Mr. President, I don't know?" replied the VP.

"You don't seem to know much lately," said the President.

"Not much to know just now, Mr. President."

"Are you fuckin' with me?"

"No, Mr. President."

"You sure?"

"Yes, Mr. President."

"Good."

On the floor of the UN, Stella turned to all the representatives as she spoke, "I have surrendered my position as the Ambassador for the United States as well as my citizenship and come here to declare and prove that the island of Wassimasiomoaki is and always has been an independent self-governing sovereign regardless of whatever claims or history may derive from the rest of the world. As such we are giving notice to the entire world that all people and nations are to stay away and leave us alone. It is not our desire to exploit any of our natural resources for money or gain. Our only desire is to live in peace with ourselves and our international neighbors.

"And just how do you support these ridiculous claims of yours?" asked the Ambassador from Israel.

"Far better than your pathetic bogus claim six months ago, Mr. Ambassador," replied Stella.

"If you have surrendered your official status here then you have no right to be here making all these claims," said the French Ambassador.

"Oh, I have every right, French Ambassador, as the official ambassador of my new country. And in fact I have a message for you and your country. There is a very, very large unused nuclear bomb buried on our island and it is leaking radioactive uranium. It is your bomb, Mr. Ambassador, a French bomb, and it has been there since 1958 and as we speak here today your country is being levied a fine of fifty million dollars and ordered to retrieve it and cleanse the ground where it's buried," said Stella.

"You cannot do this," said the French Ambassador. "There is no record of such a thing."

"Oh get a clue there muffin maker. And since you want evidence, then I tell you the evidence is with the people who live on that island and for that very purpose I have brought you the grandson of Hooky Chua Latta, King Popo YoYo, Chief and Top Coconut Jam, Bread Fruit, and Funglu Distributor in Perpetuity."

Popo YoYo walked to the center of the room, threw open and removed his long silver/white fur coat to reveal a dark tanned naked muscular man wearing nothing but a loin cloth, a bead necklace, and a Mickey Mouse watch he had gotten when Stella took him to Disneyland. He especially liked the roller coaster and rode it no less than 14 times. Everyone at the UN gasped, (especially the women). Some rose in protest, some even laughed. "I am Popo YoYo, the humble King of Wassimasiomoaki Island and leader of my people who have since the first days of the earth *have* always and always *will* reside there. We have never been or will ever be claimed by any other people and all that is our island is ours and ours alone."

During the past six months Stella had been teaching Popo YoYo how to speak English and had also rehearsed him on what he was now saying and as he was saying it she hoped like hell he would stick to the script.

"May I repeat," said Popo YoYo. *"We have never legally been or will ever be claimed by any other people and all that is our island is ours and ours alone. Therefore I say to all the world, stay the fuck away from my island!"*

Stella was shocked. Her good student, Popo YoYo, had found his English language independence perhaps a little too well, but... what the hell, it seems to be working.

"Wow, that guy must really work out. All muscle and no fat. Guess they don't have a McDonalds there on, uh, Thingamajig Island," observed the President.

"To hell with that guy. What about Stella? Is she hot or what?" said the VP.

"Who? Stella? Hah, yeah she's a hotty, but you might as well pocket that idea my dear Vice President. That girl's door swings the wrong way."

"What's her door got to do with anything?"

"Shit. Where do they find you politicians?"

Chapter 36

Home at Last

By the time Stella and Popo YoYo had returned home the United Nations elected to recognize the small island of Wassimasiomoaki as an independent nation, mostly because she had threatened to expose Wambaga's New York sex life to the rest of the world and especially to his four wives, two of which were former Watusi warriors who often express serious bouts of jealousy which had the potential to turn lethal. Faced with this and having a hard enough time trying to explain his deal with Somali pirates, Wambaga wasted no time encouraging the members of the UN to grant recognition and national status to the Honorable King Popo YoYo and the Island of Wassimasiomoaki. Wambaga was soon removed shortly after and it was rumored he was now living with pirates in Somalia after escaping violent protesting crowds in his own country.

Before leaving the US, Stella had taken Popo YoYo to the White House where she negotiated a treaty whereby the United States would provide military protection for the next 100 years without ever placing one foot on the island. For this service the islanders would provide regular supplies of funglu which it turns out only a small dose was not only a super aphrodisiac but a cure-all for a number of diseases and the effects of radiation exposure. Of course the President and a number of his Cabinet members shared business interest in the distribution of their newly discovered drug named *funglux*. Of course the islanders kept the funglu formula secret.

Stella came home with a few gifts which made the lives of the newly arrived island residents a little more pleasurable. For Captain Robert E. Lee Fairfield she brought a Fender guitar so he could pursue his rock and roll dream and a few other instruments such as drums and horns for anyone who cared to join him. The result was a great show at the new Black Ass Bar each Saturday night. For the Black Ass gang she managed to get her hands on 24 cases of Three Horses Beer when she stopped off to make arrangements to ship home the body of their deceased fellow deserter Samson Chillea whose remains had been stuck in the Black Ass bar freezer for eight months. For Corky, who had taken on the position of school teacher with his assistant Sammytu to interpret, Stella brought a wide variety of books. She wasn't quite sure what to get the Chinese boys so she picked up six cases of soy sauce, six cases of teriyaki, and four Mahjong games. For all the men on the island she bought an endless supply of Speedos of various colors and patterns and for every villager on the island she brought New England Patriots baseball hats, knowing that anything else she would get them to wear would never get worn. There were assorted presents for others that were intended to match their likes and personalities such as 20 cans of Georgia boiled peanuts for T-Bone, pizza makings for Nino, and the special gift of a radio with three years worth of batteries for the little Priestess. Though these gifts made Stella feel good it also made her feel guilty and worry that it was the beginning of the end of a beautiful society, but she had to admit to herself that someday somehow all things must come to an end and slowly, hopefully ever so slowly, these people would have to be prepared.

On the first night home the entire population of the island sat around the village center and listened to Popo YoYo speak of his great adventure in the other world but on the second night they dealt with politics and the only thing on the agenda was a name. Though it wasn't a problem for the original islanders, the very name *Wassimasiomoaki* was just too damn hard for anyone else in the world to pronounce, therefore the entire political discussion on this night consisted of everyone trying to agree on a new name. All kinds of names were suggested from all nationalities in all kinds of languages. The entire process was becoming tedious and tiresome. There were American names of people and places and there were Chinese names of people and places many of which were just as hard to pronounce. Some names popped up from the original islanders but most of those were just as difficult to pronounce as Wassimasiomoaki. Eventually names were beginning to be discarded and some of the few that were left following the process of elimination were names such as Sea Breeze, Salty Dog, Cheeseburger, Disco, Coney Island West, Singapore More, and Charlie Town. Everyone agreed these were all bad names.

Part of the process of selecting names went as follows; when someone would suggest a name like maybe *Shoe* and Sammytu would turn to Slammin' Sammy and say, "Shoe good name?" and Slammin' Sammy would shake her head no and then Sammytu would yell, "Shoe bad name!" and everyone would agree and they would start all over. While they were going through the final list of names, Chow Chow, who had finally landed his short island woman, sat watching and sipping his funglu. When he realized his cup was empty he turned to his girl and called out *funglu* and Sammytu turned to Slammin' Sammy and said "*Funglu* good word? I think funglu good word." Slammin' Sammy thought a moment then nodded her head in agreement and Sammytu quickly shouted out, "FUNGLU GOOD NAME!"

So there it was, the new name of Wassimasiomoaki Island had just been officially changed to *The Isle of Funglu.* By the time the former yacht Yellow Rose returned for the first time, Stella and Corky had drawn up official documents announcing the island's new name and sent them to the United Nations, the White House, the

State Department, and Rand McNally. A few days later there was the only other political decision to be made for the next 10 years and it wasn't made in a democratic manner. It came when Popo YoYo brought all the people together and announced that he, as king of The Isle of Funglu, declared there would be built a bodacious roller coaster at the base of the mountain. And so it came to pass that they did exactly that. With a fist full of diamonds Popo YoYo contracted the Disney Company to build his roller coaster.

When the French came to collect Hooky's big egg they were perplexed as to what to do with Hooky. They were amazed when the islanders just strolled up to the Big Kahuna pole, threw Hooky onto a rack and strolled off, all without anti-radioactive suits. When they expressed concerns over the safety of those involved the islanders simply smiled and offered them some funglu of which the Frenchmen politely declined, preferring instead their own wine. "They'll never know what they missed," said Nino Bambino.

It took the French less than a week to clean up the big egg mess and soon after Hooky and the Big Kahuna memorial were moved to the top of the mountain where he rest to this day watching over his people and his island.

 Epilogue

It was a wonderful balmy Pacific day with few clouds, a bright sun, and a steady soft breeze crossing over the island. The surf drifted onto the sandy beach, exotic birds sang from beyond the swaying palm trees and all was right with the world. Tarabi, the young pump man pirate, ambled along the beach without a care in the world, whistling and tossing small shells and stones into the water, and contemplating just how lucky he was not to be back in Somalia, when down the beach he saw something big wash ashore. When he finally strolled up to it and examined it closely he realized it was a young man on a makeshift raft. The man was weak, worn, sunburned, hungry, and beaten by many months floating alone and surviving in the ocean, but he still had enough energy to turn and look up and smile.

Tarabi smiled in return and said, "As-Salaam-Alaikum."

The young Iranian Republican Guard soldier held his painful smile and said, "Wa-Alaikum-Salaam."

On the very far end of the island where few people ever go is a small stack of rocks covering a bag of bones belonging to Tex the Big Bopper of the Texas Yellow Rose Corporation. His bones were placed there by the Black Ass boys after he was hosted at an island luau complete with lots of roasted pig, fish, coconut jelly, bread fruit, bananas, and Christmas holiday funglunog. Everyone agreed that for a very nasty man he didn't taste half bad.

About the author 🌴

Frank Mosco is the author of ten books which include eight novels. He is a native of Annapolis, Maryland, who now lives and writes in Florida. Frank began collecting awards for writing while still in high school, then again as a journalist in college where he majored in Broadcast Management & Media. He went on to produce material for all forms of media as a reporter, columnist, producer, director, and photographer, as well as media and communications work for the Federal Government and the White House. After many years on the beaches of Florida, which influenced a number of his books, he now produces mostly fictional novels of which he says, *"...can be just as strange as reality but far more convenient and definitely more fun."*